The Bookshop
of Panama

The Bookshop of Panama

Suzanne Hope

The Book Guild Ltd

First published in Great Britain in 2019 by
The Book Guild Ltd
9 Priory Business Park
Wistow Road, Kibworth
Leicestershire, LE8 0RX
Freephone: 0800 999 2982
www.bookguild.co.uk
Email: info@bookguild.co.uk
Twitter: @bookguild

This work is entirely fictitious and bears no resemblance to any persons living or dead.

Typeset in Adobe Garamond Pro

Printed and bound in Great Britain by CPI Group (UK) Ltd, Croydon, CR0 4YY

ISBN 978 1912881 154

British Library Cataloguing in Publication Data.
A catalogue record for this book is available from the British Library.

MIX
Paper from
responsible sources
FSC® C013604
FSC
www.fsc.org

For my mother Sylvia Hope, who gifted me the love of books and always selflessly encouraged me to do the things that made me happy, wherever they took me in the world.

ACKNOWLEDGMENT

Thanks to Francesco for the never-ending support. Thanks also to Sandra for help with editing and for her friendship, advice and for countless fun nights at *Oasi della Birra* in Rome – talking books and not much else.

With credit: GettyImages/omersukrugoksu

Kate's Notes on Panama – from Internet Research

Central America – Remember: Mr. Dean's geography class (failed!). Links North and South America. Bridge of the America's? What's that?

Panama hat – from Ecuador – what!!?? Panama Canal – OK interesting – but not that interesting? (Can study up on Central American history…)

Narrow – 120 miles wide at most. Will need a car? Beaches? Yes! Caribbean and Pacific Oceans – Yeah!! Clothes: need new swimwear, flip-flops, shorts. Umbrella? Hat! 50 factor sun cream!!!!

Colombia on the southern border! Yikes!! Dangerous? Drugs and kidnapping!?

Good things: Just 2 hours to Miami and 4 to New York (great bookshops!), lots of English, tropical fruit, fresh fish, rum cocktails, cheap – compared to London, no Hurricanes or earthquakes, non-stop flights to Europe. (But 11hrs!) Relatively safe (apparently?).

Bad things: salsa (!!!), Humid!!! (Frizzy hair! Need extra strength Frizz Ease!). No seasons. Always hot. Rains a lot. Spanish – will have to learn it – and I'm crap at languages. No friends. Not that many bookshops???! Shit – no bookshops?????

"There is no frigate like a book to take us lands away."

Emily Dickinson

1

"We live as we dream – alone..."

Heart of Darkness, Joseph Conrad

Panama. I never imagined I would end up living here. Strange, isn't it? You know, how things work out. I didn't even know where Panama was until I looked it up on a map.

I've been here two months and fourteen days – Yes, I'm counting the days – And I'm beginning to wonder if I could go mad from the heat. As far as I know, there have never been any known cases of insanity in my family, but I could always be the first. Temperatures are scorching, but it's the humidity which gets to you, wrapping itself around you – oppressive and muggy, clinging to you each and every day. I'm covered in an ever-present veil of sweat and can't get rid of it – no matter how many cold showers I take. And believe me, I've tried.

Today I'm feeling lethargic and low and I'm lying on the sofa. The ceiling fan is wafting hot air around and I'm watching a small leaf green lizard on the living room ceiling. He – I decided he's a boy from the beginning – is often around. He seems the only thing alive around here impervious to the roasting temperatures and right now he's making a light lunch out of a small cluster of mosquitoes. He has become my close companion. We are sharing this living space and our lives together these days – it's me and him, the mosquitoes, my books and now a little writing too.

And here they are – my words and thoughts on the pages you're reading. I'm writing for me – and for the abstract you. Maybe I should introduce myself. I'm Kate Lewis. I'm not going to give you a physical description right now. I'll skip that, but what I will tell you is why I ended up here in Panama. And I'm hoping that getting my story down on my laptop where I can see it will somehow help me make sense of what's happened and where I might end up next.

Where to start? I guess there are many places to start a story but as I'm feeling uninspired, let's take today. It's been a day just like every other – it usually goes like this: emails to friends, searching Amazon.com for a new book, reading, checking my bank balance online, FB, Instagram and more reading. When I have the will power, I'm becoming a master at superficial home improvements too: re-arranging my books, hanging pictures, or simply re-organizing the things on my kitchen shelves. In London, this "pottering" would have been done in pajamas and was generally a Sunday afternoon affair. Here, it's far too hot and sticky for pajamas and every day seems like Sunday to me.

I guess the one good thing about being here in Panama, in my unusual situation, is the time I have to read. I've just finished *Daughter of Fortune* by Isabel Allende. In spite of our differences I felt some strange empathy with the main character Eliza. She's from Chile in South America and I'm from Lancashire, England, but we both went in search of something across the seas, and well, it didn't turn out at all as we expected, not for either of us. Her story starts with a baby in a wicker basket in Chile in the 1800s; mine, 200 years later on a very wet, average Saturday afternoon in a London pub over a lunchtime pint and with an order of chicken and chips in a basket instead.

October last year, it was damp and drizzling and I was waiting for Marco in my favorite pub the Blue Flag in Covent Garden,

London. We'd had a good two hours shopping; Marco, to Oxford Street in search of CDs; me, to Covent Garden where I'd spent an hour hunting for an outfit for a friend's wedding. Clothes shopping on a busy Saturday afternoon wasn't my favorite pastime, so with nothing to show for my troubles except a mild headache and the beginnings of a depression about how much weight I'd gained, I headed for the bookshops on Charing Cross Road – battling the showers and dodging the puddles on the way.

In spite of today's dreadful weather, this was still my favorite time of the entire week. Here, I could slip into an Ian Rankin crime novel, historical fiction, autobiography, or the latest bestseller – no problem. All these book jackets fit me perfectly. You see, I'm a bit of a bookworm. I love books. Books aren't just a hobby, they're a big part of my life: hardback, softback, second-hand, brand-new, fiction, non-fiction. I've always got a book in my bag wherever I go, a pile by my bed, a comforting book somewhere with the corner turned down pausing on the page, expectantly waiting for me to read on.

I've been a bookworm since I was eight. Each summer my mother and I would spend a two-or three-week holiday at my grandfather's house in York in the north of England. My grandfather was a retired head school teacher and I guess he'd had enough of children as he had become a little grumpy and intolerant of them in his old age, no exception made for me. He spent many hours in his garden in the summer, smoking his pipe and pottering in his vegetable plot and while he did I'd sneak into his dank, dusty, disused study at the back of the house.

I loved this room. It felt as if the room hadn't been cleaned since my grandma died three years before – and it probably hadn't – but the place fascinated me with is yellowing lace curtains, high wooden shelves, old leather-bound books, boxes of documents, newspapers and magazines. Everything you touched was covered in a layer of thick, nebulous dust. The smell of stale pipe smoke still hung in the air. I'd spend what seemed like hours inspecting the many old leather-bound books – most of them were incomprehensible, one ancient looking encyclopedia of insects with detailed diagrams particularly fascinating. But then I found old copies of the C. S. Lewis classic, *The Chronicles of Narnia*. Given that most of my grandfather's books were unreadable to me, these books were an unexpected find so, in spite of the fact that they were falling apart, brittle bits of flaking tape holding many of the loose pages in place, I was undeterred.

Once I'd discovered the Narnia books, each day I crept across the creaking floor boards and slipped inside the study, read a few pages then tip toed out again with a flush of excitement. I had discovered the world of Narnia and was reading it in secret! I didn't know if I was doing something wrong; that is, if the study was out of bounds, perhaps. Nobody had told me it was, but it felt like it was and this uncertainty made the whole thing more fun, more exciting, more Narnia.

For a long time after, I thought that my Narnia reading days were my secret alone, but when my grandfather died many years later, my mother phoned me up in Cambridge and told me that she had spoken to the lawyer and unexpectedly my grandfather had willed me half of his estate and (strangely) an old set of C. S. Lewis's Narnia books. I realized there and then that he had known what I had been doing all along. Perhaps in an odd kind of way he had encouraged the whole thing.

The Chronicles of Narnia changed me forever. My nickname at school soon became the less than flattering "Bog-eyed Bookworm." Each morning and afternoon break, when the other children were heading out to the school yard to play, I'd make for the limited school library. I soon started a collection of my own with the money I earned from a paper round and began venturing off to discover the delights of the bookshops in Lancaster and its surrounds.

I see myself now. I'm the small, quiet, red-haired child at the back of the bookshop. It's Saturday afternoon and I'm sitting on a small wooden stool, surrounded by books and lost to the world around me. The sun is shining outside, but I'm oblivious as I've just discovered Emily Brontë and I'm in love with Heathcliff. I'm full to the brim with the notion of windswept moors, of passionate love and the young woman who wrote it. I take the book to the counter and count out the pound coins. The assistant is kind and she knows me by now, but I'm too shy to engage in her friendly banter. I'm fourteen.

Since none of my school mates shared the passion, I became a rather solitary child and it wasn't until I earned a place at university that I really made any friends. At Cambridge a whole new world opened up to me. Apart from occasional holidays with my parents and to my grandfather's house each summer I'd lead a pretty sheltered life. I was the first of the Lewis family to get a university education and Cambridge expanded my horizons overnight. It was a daunting experience for a shy, self-contained just turned 18-year-old but I suffered the stresses and strains of the first year, made a few friends and gradually settled down to the routine of college life.

At first, I thought I was in heaven, with the studious atmosphere, impeccable libraries, surrounded by seemingly like-minded people but over time, all was not well. I loved books, they were my passion but studying at Cambridge reduced my passion to a methodical process of dissection, analysis and theory. Over the three years, this methodical and passionless approach gradually sucked the enthusiasm out of me. I emerged with an average degree and the resolution never to study literature in that way again. Oh, what joy to just pick up a book purely for the enjoyment of reading it!

So back to London and this average wet Saturday afternoon where I've chosen to begin my story…

I'd cut my shopping trip short due to the persistent drizzle and was treating myself to a beer in the Blue Flag. I was drying off my glasses and trying not to think about how I still had to find something to wear to the wedding. I made a resolution to start the diet on Monday.

On the positive side, I had six new books sitting in an inviting pile on the table. I picked up the first, a quality hardback copy of *Oliver Twist*. I felt the smooth dust jacket in my palm and opened the book at page one. The paper was thick and solid in my fingers and the perfume of this paper-bound treasure subtle and reassuring. I'd read this book three times already, but no matter, as one of my favorites I deserved a quality copy and *Oliver Twist* himself deserved no less.

I checked my phone for messages. Nothing. Marco must be on his way. My mind went back to the pile of books in front of me. For a moment the surge of excitement they offered slipped out of my grasp with a touch of guilt. *Oliver Twist* was one thing, but in truth, maybe I didn't need the illustrated copy of Carl Sagan's *Cosmos*. After all, I already had the paperback and what I needed more was a new pair of shoes. My trainers suddenly felt very soggy and looking down on them now, I had to admit they looked shabby too. I made a mental note: Next Saturday no books, new trainers. It was a note I'd made to myself many times before.

Marco had just arrived and was waving. I signaled that I already had a drink and watched him across the crowded, noisy lunchtime bar getting served. His hair and jacket were dripping and I could see he was hunched over in a vain attempt to keep the damp from his skin.

Marco was half Italian and he often said that he'd never get used to English weather – I think he'd had too many long childhood summer holidays in Sardinia, soaking up the Mediterranean sun. He came over, smiling, Guinness spilling down the side of his glass. Marco always had been a touch on the clumsy side.

"What have you got there?" I asked knowingly reaching up for his carrier bags and smiling as he sat down.

"Oh, just a few new CDs," he grinned pulling out a chair, passing it over the table, taking a sip from the top of his glass and eyeing up the books on the table. I often thought Marco didn't look half Italian at all. He had thick, dark blond hair which he kept short in a crew cut and chestnut eyes. His family, all from Milan, were dark but the fairer, rugged complexion of his Cornish father had made its mark on him for sure. Today, he looked as English as a member of the royal family in spite of his scruffy denim jacket and jeans. Yes, he was a good-looking guy and deep down, I always wondered whether he was just a bit too good-looking for me.

"Kate! More books? Really, haven't you already got a huge pile of unread books at home?! Where are you going to put them all? The shelves are overflowing, and more to the point, when are you going to find time to read them?"

As much as he'd tried, Marco never really understood my fascination with books. He was a do-er; I, more the reader out of the two, but I couldn't complain, he was usually supportive when I blatantly over-spent on books and rarely grumbled about my books taking over our small London flat which, I had to admit, they were. Living room, bedroom, kitchen, even bathroom. Each room had its fair share of books and I desperately needed to put up more shelves to host the growing pile by our bed.

"And did you find anything for Jen's wedding?"

"No, 'fraid not. But I've got one last chance on Thursday after work next week and if I don't find anything I'll just wear the same dress that I wore to Mark's. Anyway, you can't say anything," I grinned back. "The only man on the planet still buying CDs!"

I opened up his bag and was going through his latest purchases when I came across a compilation of salsa classics from Central America.

"Never been mad on salsa…" I admitted rather grudgingly "… after all, one track sounds just like the rest. Now this Miles Davis CD looks good…"

"Kate, I've been meaning to tell you all day, I was just waiting for the right time, the new postings list came around – and I'm down for Panama."

"Really, Panama? When did you find out about that?" My glass was only half empty but hearing this news I was suddenly beginning to feel like it was time to order another drink.

"Err, Tuesday. Anyway, I know it's a lot to take in," he said over the top of his Guinness, "but we do need to consider it. It's only the first post that's come up on the list but it might not be a bad one and if I don't accept this, the next postings might be Khartoum or Dakar and then what would we do? I mean, considering that you're not keen to go to the deep field…"

He pulled over the menu card, wiped the white Guinness moustache from his mouth and studied it.

"Deep Field". I always thought that sounded such pretentious United Nations jargon. What they really meant by deep field was "in the middle of nowhere in a developing country surrounded by poverty, starvation and maybe even life-threatening violence" – not a bookshop in site either, erm, no, not too keen on that at all. Oblivious to my racing thoughts, Marco went on.

"So, I asked around at work," he said putting the menu card down and studying my face. "Everyone in the office said Panama is great, an easy place to live, I mean, I think you'd like it. It's developed – it'd be much easier to live in than somewhere like the Sudan or Congo. Of course, there aren't many emergencies over there, but at least I'd get a bit closer to the field again. Anyway, let me get a food order in then we can talk. What would you like?"

While he was back at the bar ordering chicken and chips in a basket for two and another round of drinks, I tried to calm my thoughts. I'd known this was going to come up sooner or later but I had been dreading it – if truth be told. Marco had worked for the UN for 12 years and was married to the cause. He was a press officer by profession, but had cut his teeth covering humanitarian emergencies in Africa. After over nine years spent right where the action was in field offices, he had worked the last three in UN regional and head offices in Hong Kong, Geneva and now London – and hated it. Hated the paperwork, hated the bureaucracy, and hated being removed from what he saw as the "real work" – saving lives. For someone like me, who craved safety, routine and all my home comforts, it was hard to imagine why, but he'd once told me working in emergencies was like being a drug addict. Once you had it in your blood, it was hard to get it out of your system.

We had met in Geneva just over a year ago at an international communications and fundraising conference.

It was the evening after a long day of seminars and talks and people had started getting drunk in the hotel bar, including me. Something to do with spending three days locked in hotel conference rooms talking nothing but communication cycles, creative content and supporter data bases. I was sitting at the bar on a high stool with my second pint of beer texting a friend back in London. Melodie was having a horrible blind date at a trendy Indian restaurant in Soho and seemed to need to share it with me in real-time. The guy had turned out to be a "complete moron" as she put it. She seemed particularly put-out when the bill came to £120 and he expected her to split it evenly. A night out with a loser and 60 quid for the experience – sometimes, being single was no fun, no fun at all.

It was a blunt reminder which I didn't need after two pints of strong Belgium wheat beer and a lonely hotel bedroom on the horizon. It was right then that Marco came up and introduced himself and I, about to order my third beer, came right out with the question that had been burning in the back of my mind since I'd spotted him across the room earlier that day: "So, where's your girlfriend, isn't she a communication guru like you, too?"

He laughed loudly and tried to get the attention of the barman. I suddenly felt like a complete fool. I'd never been forthright with the opposite sex and now that I had given it a try, I'd made a complete idiot of myself.

At the age of 35, I had only managed to have a couple of long-term boyfriends. Peter was the first and most significant. It had lasted just over a year and had ended, together with university, when Peter had wanted to take a year out traveling but I'd wanted to get established with a job in London. I had always, secretly, regretted that decision, just a little bit. I got together with the second, Alex, at a Christmas office party. But over time it was clear he was more into his vinyl collection than he was into me. It had been like living in a bad version of *High Fidelity* by Nick Hornby, so I'd kicked him into touch at the repeat office Christmas party a year later.

"I'm not a guru and I don't have a girlfriend. Why? You interested?" Marco grinned right back. He was certainly confident and had more than just a mischievous grin to be confident about. I won't say that it won me over there and then, but my heart skipped a beat and I wanted to find out more, and to my surprise, he seemed interested to talk to me too. We hung out in the bar and over drinks chatted about the conference and work including a recent assignment he'd just done in Bangkok. He came across as so different from me – adventurous and experienced. He had lived in so many places too – it was hard to keep up with all the details. Maybe it's true that opposites attract. Even back then, I had to admit, I was aware that in many ways he wasn't my ideal man. He smoked roll ups, didn't read fiction and hated living in big cities like London, but I couldn't deny it: he had something. So I couldn't help being more than surprised and delighted when at the end of the conference he asked me for my number.

The following Sunday, I got back to London, tired and a little deflated. I'd only just finished unpacking and was feeling depressed by the mountain of laundry growing in the basket and the assumption that I'd never see him again, when the phone rang. It was Marco. We chatted a while and before long had a date fixed for the very next night. Dirty socks and M&S undies could wait.

I saw him almost every night that week and we moved in together six months later. It was the most reckless thing I'd ever done. Now, a year down the line, we were engaged. No date set for the wedding but that was only a matter of time.

That non-descript hotel bar in Geneva seemed a very long time ago now, and here I was, sitting over yet another beer in another city, with images of Panama City and a bad salsa rhythm on my mind. I made a mental note "scrap new trainers – add Panama Guide Book to book list".

Marco, back from the bar, started talking about how he was sure I'd be able to get a job there. He had already looked into it and lots of local charities had offices in Panama.

"Why don't you start looking? You know I'd feel much more comfortable about this if you had a job, too. You'd have to learn Spanish of course but…"

"Marco, you're really moving fast! Give me a chance for it to sink in! I mean, this is just the first possible posting, right? You don't have to accept it do you?"

"Sure, I don't have to accept, but you know how the UN rotation system works Kate. They'll only give me a chance at three or four positions and if I don't accept any of them, I could be out of a job. And as I said, especially for you, seeing as you're not keen on going to Africa, well Panama could be a good option. It's developed, safe, and close to the US…"

"OK but Marco, give me a chance to take it in. All I know about Panama is that there's a canal and it's famous for hats. I don't even know where it is on the map, and you want us to move there, just like that!"

As soon as the words were out, I felt wretched. He wasn't being pushy or unreasonable and I knew it. Marco had already stayed in London longer than he'd wanted to – for me. I knew he was secretly itching to get closer to the action, back to the field and I guessed even Panama was a compromise for him. He had recently met up with colleagues back on home leave from the Congo and had been restless all that week after hearing their stories. I studied his face and posture, he looked just ever so slightly deflated, like a party balloon the day after a children's birthday party that is starting to go a bit flat.

"Look Kate, we'll only go if this is a good move for both of us. I can always look for another job…"

"Come on, you love working for the UN," I interrupted. He gave me a weak smile.

"Well, I guess if you could consider it… I do really need to get something where I'm not stuck in an office day after day. It's driving me nuts! And then there's all the internal politics, the bureaucracy… I don't know how much more I can take!" We were silent for a moment. Marco looked tired, drawn.

"I need a cigarette. Just popping outside for a quick smoke. Won't be long," he said, getting up and searching in his pockets for his cigarettes and lighter.

While he was gone I gazed out of the window and tried to collect my thoughts. The rain had stopped but the streets outside were still damp, gloomy and deserted, except for a small number of resolute shoppers and the occasional black cab. In contrast, the pub was dry and bright, the atmosphere merry. I sipped my beer and glanced around, feeling so at home and at ease in this snug and familiar setting. With this backdrop, it was hard to conjure up images of Panama, a land so far away, so poles apart. It was even tougher to picture what life would be like there. I had always loved my routine, craved security and stability. It was a lot for me to digest – adventure was not my thing, but in spite of this, two things were clear: Number one, Marco deserved my support. Number two, I really, absolutely did not want to end up in what the UN considered a "hard duty station" like Sudan.

Maybe I just had to take the bit by the teeth. Marco was back, smelling of cigarettes and with moisture from the damp atmosphere of the late afternoon clinging to his hair. He sat down and sipped his beer silently.

"Of course, I'll consider it Marco." He looked up and scrutinized my face.

"Look, I'm sorry for being so negative, it's just that Panama is such a long way away and I can't quite imagine it right now. Hey, how about we eat out tonight? We haven't treated ourselves in ages and we can discuss it over dinner. I just have to get my head around things. You know me, I need to warm up to new ideas – it takes me a bit of time, and this is… well, let's just say I certainly have to get my head around it…" I was trying to sound positive but was beginning to ramble. Marco leaned over the table and gave my hand a tight squeeze.

"*Amore.* I understand. Don't worry. We're in this together."

2

"A companion's words of persuasion are effective"

The *Iliad*, Homer

Tropical climates are not what they are cracked up to be. Believe me. My favorite bag has gone green. It has grown mold from the humidity and it took me an hour to clean that off. After lunch, I pulled everything else out of the wardrobe and found more; one belt, two pairs of shoes and a white bag, all with patches of light green mold dotted all over like a gorgonzola cheese. I guess it's not surprising – it has been raining here every day with temperatures in the high 90s and I'd been warned about what the humidity can do to leather.

It made me think of the novel *One Hundred Years of Solitude* by Gabriel Garcia Marquez. I first read it at university and had been hooked from the first page. I remember so clearly when Garcia Marquez describes how it rains for four years, eleven months and two days. I haven't been in Panama for four years, of course. Like I said, just two months, 14 days and… six hours, but it feels like 1,000 years right now.

That's why I decided to start writing this story, my story. I've always been a reader but never a writer and I wanted to see if I could put something down on paper myself rather than just taking from the printed page all my life.

It's not easy for me. The words don't flow from my fingers like I expected them to, but it helps me pass the time and I'm hoping it will also help me understand my life and – what to do next. And anyway, how can you really appreciate good literature if you've never tried writing for yourself? It's like all those people who criticize modern art. Have you ever tried throwing paint on a canvas and making it look good? I've tried and I can tell you – it isn't as easy as you think. Same with writing. For example, where do you start? No story has a fixed beginning, middle or end. If you've read chapter one you'll have seen that I started my story in London – but I could've easily started it in Lancashire, Panama, New York or Geneva.

But today, as I sit upstairs in the mezzanine bedroom writing, and quietly sweating under the sluggish ceiling fan, I glance down to the kitchen and see the vase I glued back together just yesterday. It was the only thing broken when I unpacked.

When the truck arrived, piled high with all my possessions carefully packed and wrapped in mountains of bubble wrap I was tempted to send the whole lot back to England, but then, where to? Our old flat in Lavender Hill in London is already leased to a new tenant and my mum and dad's place in Dolphinholme near Lancaster is too small. So instead, I spent one week unpacking, unraveling, finding a home for all the useless things I used to think were important in my life.

I could see immediately that Marco had gotten to the consignment before it was shipped and removed most of his stuff. But he had obviously been in a hurry, as I came across some of his things, things he had missed in his haste. There were two pairs of shoes, five pairs of combat shorts, two Armani suits (never worn), his camera and a box of photos.

"Fancy a wine?" That's Jane shouting up to me from my kitchen.

Jane is keeping me company today as I write. She is remarkable. Jane is short, blond and very lively. She has a face which always seems ready to break into a smile and her favorite band of all time is *Earth, Wind & Fire*. She has three passions in life; wine, food and socializing and generally does them in that order. She wouldn't do well in solitary confinement – she wouldn't last 10 minutes. She'd be best friends with the guards within seconds of arriving and would soon have a dinner party with them planned for when she got out.

Talking of dinner parties, Jane is making supper tonight for some of her friends who she has invited around to my place. I know that sounds strange, but she really wants me to meet them and thinks it will do me good to get to know some other people in Panama City. I told her that I was in no mood to go out socializing but that's a concept she just doesn't understand, so in the end we've compromised at this. I have made Jane promise not to tell them about what happened with Marco. She thinks I'm being silly but I'd just feel like a total fool if they knew the details. I mean, it's embarrassing.

I met Jane in the café right around the corner from where I was staying when I first arrived in Panama City. She comes from North London and her boyfriend Chase is in Miami. Within 10 minutes of meeting, she had told me that she had been deported from the US a year earlier – all a huge mistake, something to do with being on the wrong visa. That's why she decided to make Panama her home while she and Chase work on getting her back to the States.

"Panama had to be better than being so far away, back in England!" she explained over her iced coffee. "This way Chase can come down to Panama in a couple of hours and so we get to see each other much more. And it's only temporary, you know, while we get this whole mess sorted out with US immigration."

I can see her now. It's the day I met Jane and we are sitting on sofas in the café. The sun is shining into the café behind her and she's writing an email to Chase on her laptop. My eyes are sore and red from another night of tears and no sleep but she hasn't noticed. While she writes, she tells me that Chase is the love of her life. I believe her there and then, although over coffee the next day hearing her many stories, it strikes me that she has had a few of those over the years.

I don't think I would normally become immediate friends with Jane. Nothing against Jane, but it usually takes me a while to get to know someone, to trust them. But she's such a bright and positive person, and I think the fact that we are both in Panama in uncommon circumstances, means that we have become friends quite quickly.

As I write, I can smell the cardamom and turmeric as she fries the spices in the pan for the dish she is making for tonight. The aroma immediately transports me back to London and to the day Marco told me about Panama.

That night, after too many pappadams in our local Indian restaurant 'The Bombay Bicycle', I had lain awake in bed, my head buzzing. Marco was asleep and snoring lightly next to me.

The initial apprehension about moving to Panama wasn't wearing off and I was uneasy. We'd talked and deliberated over dinner and the more I tried to be positive for Marco on the outside, the more unsure I felt on the inside.

After another hour of tossing and turning, sleep was still eluding me, so I got out of bed. It was raining hard against the bedroom window – unusual for London. I kind of liked it. The orange light from the street lamp outside gave everything in the room a strange quality; it was like seeing in black and white with a sepia tint washed over it.

My feet found my slippers on the floor and, pulling on a dressing gown, I made my way to the kitchen, switched on the kettle and opened the laptop on the table. I was wide awake and before long I'd Googled Panama and was clicking through various pages of Panama content.

I immediately found lots of websites on Panamanian real estate but eventually I found some more interesting stuff showing dream-like beaches, vibrantly exotic wildlife and the old part of town called *Casco Viejo,* which looked like a cross between Spain and Havana. One page told me that the shopping was some of the best in the region, another that Costa Rica was just up the coast and it was only four and a half hours from New York. It didn't look too bad in theory, but what would the reality be like, I wondered, squeezing out my chamomile tea bag and adding a little cold water to the cup from the tap. Granted, I was ready for a change and was most definitely burnt out at work right now, but this was such a big move. Not only that but I had never been good with heat and then there was Marco and I. We had been engaged now for six months, but were we ready for this move? It suddenly all seemed to be happening a little too fast.

The next day I met my friend Melodie for a coffee. It was a wonderfully bright late afternoon. The rain of the night before seemed to have cleaned both the air and my mind and I felt lighter and strangely more positive.

Melodie and I had met at Cambridge University. We had both been undergraduates in English Literature and over the years she had become my closest friend. In spite of an occasional brief period of losing touch after university, we had remained close ever since and had shared an ongoing passion for reading. While I had dropped into charity work, she had gone on to become a freelance writer.

"God, Kate, you've got to go for it!" she said before she had even gotten through her first mouthful of chocolate cake. We were sitting on the South Bank over coffee and huge slices of cake. London looked dazzling in the early Sunday evening sunlight – it was a poignant reminder that this was a great city and of just how much I loved it.

"It's a great opportunity to take some time out from the rat race and see another part of the world. And it's not like you're leaving your dream job behind. You've been saying for some time that you're burned out with charity fundraising. I'd definitely come and visit you and look, I'd miss you loads, but we could email and Skype each other all the time."

"But what about all that sun and the heat and well… I'll be permanently covered in sun cream and then there are the insects and…"

"Oh, Kate." She laughed. "You really should hear yourself. You sound ridiculous. You must be the only person on the planet who prefers cold wet weather to a warm sunny day."

"Well, you know what I'm like." I felt a bit embarrassed. "Remember when I got sun stroke in France?"

Melodie and I had taken a two-week holiday to the South of France three years ago. We had rented a villa just outside Cannes and had flown down, each with a pile of books. We had spent the entire holiday sitting by the pool reading with the only break being for lunch and dinner. It was one of the best holidays I had ever had except for a very bad case of sunstroke after I stayed out in the sun one day without my sun hat or cream. My fair skin had literally bubbled on my back and I had had to spend the last two days of the holiday locked in the bedroom with the shutters closed.

"I'm just not sure about moving abroad, Melodie. I really love London and to be honest I find the whole thing a bit daunting. It's hard to know if I'll even like Panama when I've never been."

"Can't you guys go over there for a visit?"

"They want a decision in the next couple weeks and Marco's at a conference all next week. There just isn't time. We have to decide next week, by the time he comes back. Oh, Melodie, what should I do, tell Marco that I want to go?"

"Well Kate, let's just say throwing caution to the wind has never been your strong point. Somehow, I wonder how you ever ended up with someone like Marco. It must be a case where opposites attract! I know he's calmed down a lot, but from what you say he used to be a bit of a UN 'action man', always off on some plane to somewhere remote, right? He sounded like the Indiana Jones of the humanitarian world before he met you!" she paused to concentrate for a second on the cake. It was very good. With another mouthful she carried on.

"I really think Panama would be good for you, good for you both – something different to experience together – a bit of an adventure. Come on, give it a chance!"

She sounded ever so slightly exasperated; I couldn't help wondering how she would feel in my shoes, quite so enthusiastic? But to be fair, she did have a point. Many people would jump at the chance to live in a tropical country for a few years. Maybe I should consider myself lucky to have such an opportunity. I sighed.

"I don't know. You could be right. And then there's Marco. You know there is only so much he can take of city life before he goes mad. To be honest, well, we haven't been getting on so well recently. Oh, just silly little arguments, but you know, Marco can be quite irritable when something's bothering him. He just hates being stuck in that office. It's depressing him and on top of that I know he thinks that I'm a bit of a stick in the mud and that I lack a sense of adventure."

Melodie frowned.

"Oh, come on Kate. You're not a stick in the mud, just very, erm, how can I say this… you are very cautious!" I had to laugh, she was right. I did lack the throw-caution-to-the-wind gene. Melodie was working her way through the cake, but somehow managed to keep talking.

"Apart from that, you told me yourself that Marco feels like he's compromised by staying in London all this time. So now maybe it's time for you to make a compromise, too." She smiled. "Live dangerously for once, and you never know, you might just surprise yourself and find out that you like it!"

Here in Panama, I miss Melodie and her practical advice, even if she got that one completely wrong. Meanwhile, Jane is putting some music on the stereo. "Are you sure this dinner is a good idea?" I venture as she hands me a glass of red wine and pours one for herself. It feels early to be drinking and she is bopping around my living room like a demented teenager at a high school disco. I suddenly feel so lost and lonely and, in a flash, I'm reminded how – in comparison to Melodie – I hardly know Jane at all. I put the wine down, and I feel a headache developing between my eyes.

"You know, I'm not sure I'm in the mood for this dinner, and what's the point of meeting new people, I don't know how long I'm going to be here and…"

"Come on Kate! You've been feeling sorry for yourself for far too long. You can't go on living the life of a hermit! Really! All you do all day is sit on your balcony, moping and feeling sorry for yourself. I'm sorry, maybe that sounds a bit harsh. I know it's hard for you right now, but try and be sociable, just for one night – see how it goes. They're a super nice, fun bunch: you'll see!"

And before I can even reply, she is bopping her way back to the kitchen, singing along to the music, making herself at home and pulling various spices out of her bag. I know she's right. It would be good for me to start going out a bit again now, making some friends. After all, I've been here for over two months and have hardly done a thing, hardly socialized with anyone. But deep down I also know that no amount of socializing and R&B music is going to make me snap out of the mood I'm in. There's only one thing to do, I grab the glass of wine and take a sip. If you can't beat them, you've just got to join them.

3

"It's a mad world. Mad as Bedlam, boy."

David Copperfield, Charles Dickens

The morning after the dinner party, I wake up with a terrible headache, a kitchen full of dirty dishes and a feeling of despondency.

What on earth am I still doing here? Why am I not on a plane back to London? I had this crazy, romantic notion that I would hang out in Panama and decide what to do with my life but it doesn't seem to be working. Instead, I'm just wallowing in self-pity and feeling worse by the day.

I check my laptop and for the first time I don't have any emails except the one from Amazon.com telling me what this summer's bestselling books are. I still haven't had the courage to get onto Skype and contact Melodie. It's easier to lie and say I'm fine by email, not so easy in front of a microphone and webcam. She would take one look at me and be here on the next flight.

Not daring to take a look at myself in the mirror – after all, I already know how bad I look – I shuffle into the kitchen to make a coffee and boil some water for an egg.

As the water is boiling I try to figure out why I'm feeling quite so low. After all, last night's dinner with Jane's friends had been much better than I had imagined. It should have cheered me up. It has been a long time since I've had company and I have to admit that it did turn into a welcome distraction. They're an entertaining, exuberant bunch and certainly know how to have a good time but I wonder what they thought of me? I tried to overcome my melancholy mood but somehow it just kept getting the better of me.

Stuart arrived first. He's short, slim and has thick, cropped brown hair. He has a Lancashire accent and I soon found out that he is from Blackpool and was an investment banker. After working for years in New York, he moved to Panama about a year ago to open up his own investment fund based on property development. Apparently, now is the right time to invest in property in Panama. If you have a spare $100,000, he soon told me, he's the one to speak with. Stuart would be a laugh a minute – if you're in the right mood. He soon made himself comfortable in my kitchen with a glass of wine, chatting to Jane as she finished preparing the dinner.

"You know, you really should buy a property here in *Casco Viejo*, Jane. Prices are going up so quickly," he said, sipping his wine. "Do you know how much property is currently going at per square meter?"

"Oh Stuart, I can't believe you're on about that again. You are property obsessed!" Jane laughed.

"Well, I just can't bear to see all these money-making opportunities going to waste. I'm looking at buying a few things myself – once the fund is up and running, that is."

"Well, good for you, Stuart," Jane smiled, toasting him with her wine before returning to stir the saucepan. "When you're a multi-millionaire let me know!"

"Oh, you won't see me for dust after that happens," he laughed in response.

Next to arrive was May from New York. The type of girl that I can find intimidating, May has Vietnamese roots and is so pretty and trendy. But I soon find out that she is not intimidating at all. Not only is she animated and gregarious but above all else incredibly warm and friendly. And I love her funky style: she arrived with her hair tied in two elaborate plaits and a bright red communist print t-shirt. I soon learn that she loves shopping in eclectic second-hand clothes stores back in the States (explaining her "look") and that she works in IT on a posting here with the UN. I resisted the temptation to ask if she had ever met a guy called Marco. That would have been too much to bear.

Beth and Nat were the last two guests to arrive. I spent most of the evening trying to figure them out. Nat is from Santa Barbara in California and seems to be a young Ernest Hemmingway type. He has a seafood business here, exporting lobster to Japan. He loves the sea and he spends most of his weekends doing underwater meditation (whatever that is), and spear fishing. He announced halfway through dinner that next week he's planning another fishing trip to Las Perlas islands and if he strikes it lucky we would all be invited to dinner at their place to eat the catch.

Beth is a much quieter character and a fair bit older than him I guess. I put her at around 52. She's from California and very "new age". I love her style – long, flowing white linen trousers and shirt with chunky amber beads. She runs the Panamanian version of Timeout called *Panorama*; it's a really popular monthly magazine here in the city. She told me that she also recently opened an all denomination "temple" right around the corner from me in the spare bedroom in their apartment where they do mediation classes and the like. They're both very "hippy" and a little intimidating. I've never really been into tree hugging and the like, but as the conversation began to flow I started to relax.

"So, Jane tells me you're here in Panama, taking some time out from the rat race?" Beth asked me as we all settled down at the table.

"That's right," I said, feeling a bit under the microscope with all the attention suddenly on me.

"So, what did you do in London?" Stuart asked pouring out more wine for everyone. It was the first time in a long time that anyone had shown any real interest in me and it was making me feel mildly uncomfortable. I shifted position in my chair to face him head on and took a sip of wine from my newly filled glass.

"Well, I was in fundraising and found I had a gap between jobs and decided to come here."

"So why Panama?" he quizzed.

"It's a long story. I'll tell you about it someday – I don't want to bore you with it now," I said smiling.

"Oh, come on. I'm sure you couldn't possibly bore us," he said kindly.

"Well, err, Panama looked pretty interesting. I thought it would be a good place to come – to try and work out my next move, that is…"

I was feeling decidedly uncomfortable about these white lies but couldn't bear the thought of explaining what happened with Marco over dinner. It would have been mortifying.

"I arrived a couple of months ago from London and well, I'm having a bit of a re-think." I continued. "I'm pretty burnt out with fundraising to be honest. I've been doing it for way too long."

"Ah, I see…" he said. "We should go out for a drink sometime – if you fancy bashing my ears about it that is. I've been in that position a couple of times myself. It's not easy."

"So, how are you finding Panama?"

"Well, I'm embarrassed to admit that I haven't seen that much of it, really. I'm just hanging out here in the city mainly – and I'm finding it difficult, to be honest. It's so different to London, to anywhere I've been before, if you know what I mean and… well, it's the first time I've been anywhere in Central America."

"Well Kate, I think you have to give it a little longer," said Beth, studying me across the table. "There's a very different vibe going on here compared to London."

"That's true," added May. "I came down here from New York, and it took me at least six months to really settle in."

Jane brought out the curry and thankfully everyone was

distracted from this conversation by the food on the table. They all started tucking in and before long the dinner was pronounced a roaring success. The conversation was jumping frantically from one topic to another and thankfully not back in my direction. One minute it was favorite restaurants in Panama, next the story of how Beth and Nat met, then Stuart's wacky business partner in New York. There was a lot of laughing, raised voices and excited interruptions. It was quite exhausting keeping up and I was happy to be a listener rather than a participating member.

"Anyone for dessert?" Jane asked, shouting from the kitchen after I had helped her clear away the empty plates and dishes. Everyone shouted a united "Yes".

"You really should join us for meditation on Wednesdays," said Beth over coffee and dessert. "I sense you're searching for something, Kate, and mediation might help. The vibe in the temple is so juicy. There's so much positive energy going on. You can feel it."

"You into snorkeling or diving, Kate?" asked Nat.

"Well, I'm not a big swimmer. I'm not very adventurous…"

"Well, if you ever want to try, I can always take you along," he said seriously.

"You know when you're down at the bottom of the reef, the world up here seems so far away. You feel really at peace and at one with the fish. It's very calming and therapeutic. You might like it and it seems a pity that you've been here all this time and still haven't yet been to the sea – I mean the real ocean – not this polluted city thing out here," he said gesticulating out of the window.

"Sure, I'd love to!" I said, trying to sound enthusiastic. Could come in handy, I thought to myself ruefully and put it in my mental calendar. Positive Energy night – Wednesdays – and underwater meditation at the weekends. They'll be signing me up to Hare Krishna next…

"Wow, this is truly divine," said Beth, suddenly changing the subject after her first bite of the tropical fruit cheese cake. "You really have to share the recipe with me, Jane."

"Sure, Beth no problem. But before we go any further, let's have a toast to Kate and welcome her to Panama!" announced Jane. Everyone picked up their glasses and there was a loud clinking of glasses in midair.

"Hear, hear!" added Stuart in a fake upper-class English accent. "Welcome to the mad house." And we all laughed. I had to admit they were a nice though pretty eclectic bunch. I couldn't help wondering if it was Panama in particular which attracted oddballs or if this group had somehow attracted each other. They were all so different but somehow seemed to really get on. You'd never normally imagine hippy Beth and Nat getting on with ex-banker Stuart. But somehow, they do.

After dinner, they all headed off to a local bar for salsa. I stayed home in spite of their protests and for the first time in a long while, pulled up some photos of Marco on my phone. I hadn't done this in weeks but I couldn't help missing him in spite of what happened, and to be frank, sometimes it just feels good to wallow in it.

I decided to tackle the washing up tomorrow and headed to bed with *David Copperfield*.

4

"It's no use going back to yesterday, because I was a different person then."

Alice's Adventures in Wonderland, Lewis Carroll

The rain stopped about an hour ago and I've just finished *Possession* by A.S. Byatt. I decide to take a walk. After finding my flip-flops under the bed, I quickly rummage through the bedside book case to find my next read. Books are my very best friends here and some days are the only company I seek. The escapism they provide is a more than welcome break and keeps my mind from wandering back to Marco and what the hell I'm doing here.

I pull out *Case Histories* by Kate Atkinson, a book I've had on my "to read" list for years, and grab my sunglasses, hat and umbrella. It's the rainy season here right now and it rains most days for a couple of hours. Afterwards, the air feels marginally fresher but before the outburst you can almost feel the water vapor hanging in the atmosphere, the pressure and the electricity waiting to discharge. But strangely enough, I'm growing to like it.

The apartment I'm renting is bearably small and sticky hot. All I have to keep cool are two lethargic ceiling fans, one in the living room and one in the mezzanine bedroom, and a freezer stocked with ice.

When I first arrived, I was staying in a cheap, impersonal chain hotel, trying to find a flat for Marco and me. Then, after Marco left, I was in a complete mess and I was about to book my ticket back to London on the next available flight but something stopped me. If you ask me what, it's hard to explain but I remember at the time that I felt that being far away from my normal setting was just what I needed. Perhaps I had some romantic notion of taking myself off to a desert island to stare at the sea and cry into a king coconut. Maybe in hindsight it was more the fear of going back to London, back to my old life only this time a life without Marco. In any case I'd only intended to stay on a couple of weeks at the most.

Then one day when I was close to booking my ticket back to London, Jane told me about her friend Andres who had just decided to go back to Argentina. His flat was available and I suddenly decided that maybe I should stay on in Panama a little longer. After all, why rush back? I had nothing to go back to – except an empty life.

I met with the landlord, a rotund jovial Panamanian with a thick head of hair and moustache. He spoke broken English with a bizarre Texan accent and was enthusiastic about me taking out a short lease. So, I've taken it on for three months. Of course, I'm not planning to be here that long. Just as long as it takes for me to pull myself together and, in the meantime, it gives me a base and a little tranquility.

I like the layout of the place, with its spiral staircase up to the bedroom and big windows overlooking a small square. I've even got a balcony where I sit and have my coffee, egg and toast in the mornings and with care I've managed to revive some of the plants which were on their last legs when I arrived. The place is screaming out for a lick of paint and there's a vague but ever persistent smell of damp, but then nothing's perfect and I'm eternally glad that it's quiet at night. The only things keeping me awake are the frequent electrical thunder storms and dreams of Marco.

The flat is in *Casco Viejo* or "Old Quarter" – and it's where I've made my temporary home. On the east edge of a sweeping bay and in direct opposition to the jagged skyline of modern high rises, *Casco Viejo* is the old colonial part of town, an odd cocktail of derelict shells, squats and beautifully restored two- and three-story buildings. A mixture of narrow, cobbled streets and squares punctuated by historical churches, old ruins and what look like overgrown, derelict bomb sites. It's a fascinating place to explore. It feels like a mini Havana and you can see most of it in a 30-minute stroll but that's fine for me, I feel like I can manage this space and I need "bite-size" right now.

As I come down from my flat to the street, the heat and humidity envelop me like a warm, moist blanket and for a moment I feel dizzy from the sheer weight of the air combined with the blistering heat. The sun is directly above my head but in spite of this I persist with my walk, feeling thankful that I remembered my sunglasses and hat. I'm not going in any particular direction, it's just an aimless stroll.

Although Panama is relatively new to me, there's already something comfortingly familiar about this neighborhood. Maybe it's because it has community, maybe it's the European feel. Sometimes I forget I'm in Central America but imagine I'm instead in some long forgotten Spanish town on the Southern Mediterranean, but then the sound of some wildly exotic tropical bird breaks the silence and there's no doubt. I'm a long way from home.

I have only been here a short time but I already recognize many of the locals who nod a friendly "*Hola*" as I pass. There's Alejandro, the guy who sits on the main street selling a strange collection of things – cigarettes, tobacco, salt, sweets and potatoes. He's always there with his vibrant green parrot who sits patiently next to him in a badly made wire cage. There's the guy on the square who makes a few cents from helping visitors find a parking space, not to mention the guy I give my change to for helping me grab a cab. On each and every road there's a building undergoing renovation with the sound of banging and drills at work and around the corner there's the original Tailor of Panama. And I'm not talking John le Carré. This guy's shop is nothing more than a room facing the narrow street and he sits every day with the door open to the pavement, working away patiently on his battered Singer sewing machine. It's a constant reminder that I'm living shoulder to shoulder with Panamanians many of whom eke a living on a few dollars a day.

Wherever I go, the streets are full of kids playing with whatever they can find turned into a toy. Stray dogs and cats abound, the cats hiding timidly up alleys, in doorways or under a car when I pass. Only a few are bold enough to approach, hoping for a tit-bit by rubbing my legs, the others preferring their usual scavenging in the many rubbish bags left out on the street corners. It always seems full of life here, the tropical vegetation taking hold in every nook and cranny, the animals, the insects, birds and strays and of course the people with their ever-present love of salsa music, but in the same breath, there's nothing frenetic in the passing of time which flows in a languid manner from each day to the next. And on Sunday, everything is enveloped in a certain stillness – even the cats and dogs it seems are taking their Sunday afternoon siesta then.

Today I decide to take a look in the main cathedral which is at the top end of the central square. It's always lively here with locals taking a leisurely walk, street venders selling Panamanian snacks and scruffy kids kicking balls around. The white façade and two bell towers dominate the plaza and as I climb the steps to enter I feel an immediate relief from the blazing sun as I walk through the pool of shadow it casts. Its high white walls and ceilings give it a grandness which complements its simplicity and I'm surprised by just how enormous it is. I don't know why, I'm not particularly religious, but I buy and light a slender white candle and place it on one of the many side altars and sit on a

31

dark, well-worn wooden pew to watch it burn. Somehow, I find it strangely comforting, relaxing.

Hitting the heat on the main square as I leave, I decide that it would be better to take a longer walk later when the evening air is cooler. As often, there's a strong sea breeze which provides a minimal restpite from the heat and the usual crowd of vultures are circulating high up on the ever-present thermals, but today it feels a few degrees warmer than usual. I can see that clouds are forming. I'm still not used to the concept of warm rain and in spite of the fact that I remembered my umbrella I head back to my local square, order a beer and take shade under one of the big sun umbrellas.

The waiter Ricky has taken a liking to me. He's always pleased to see me and flirts outrageously even though he knows that I've noticed the ring on his wedding finger. I start reading my new book to try and avoid the constant grins he's throwing my way between serving customers.

I've already downed my first beer and am on the fourth chapter when, for a moment, I think I see Marco on the other side of the square. Then almost in the same instant I realize that of course it's not him, Marco wouldn't have the nerve to set foot in Panama right now after what he did to me, even if the job of UN Secretary General was riding on it.

Preparing for the move had gone relatively smoothly. I'd handed in my notice both at work and with our landlord in Lavender Hill and had been up to Dolphinholme to say goodbye to my mum and dad. Before I knew it, we'd already contracted the international removal company and I was out on my work leaving do in a trendy bar in Central London. I had been sad to say goodbye to my small bunch of colleagues and friends from the office, but next day I already felt better and ready for what was ahead. I was doing fine and so strangely enough my main concern became Marco. As the move date approached he seemed more stressed than ever. He told me he was overwhelmed with all the things he had to get done before leaving. He was staying in the office later and later each evening to get everything done.

Marco is sitting at our table in the kitchen. It's late. He's tired and silent as he takes a bite from the dinner I prepared earlier for him. He looks over and smiles weakly. "I'm shattered. I need to get to bed. I have another early start tomorrow." He gives me a hug and makes for the bathroom. By the time I join him in bed he is already soundly asleep. I switch on my reading light and wonder where Marco is in his dreams. Is he with me?

Then the bombshell.

"I've got to go to Sudan," he said as soon as we'd kissed each other hello.

It was two weeks before we were due to leave London for Panama and I was meeting Marco near his office at Warren Street underground station. It was a bitterly cold February evening and the tube entrance was particularly windy. People were huddled in one corner, waiting for friends, husbands, wives, like penguins in a BBC nature documentary. I was on the other side and almost frozen solid but at the news my cheeks flushed hot with a wave of nausea and panic.

I had been dragging him to a book signing by a new and up-and-coming author in a nearby independent book store but that was quickly off the agenda, given his news and instead we headed for a nearby tapas bar across the road to talk.

The bar was quiet with just one other couple smooching over cocktails as we came in with a blast of winter air, our eyes adjusting to the dim, slightly reddish light. We ordered two glasses of wine and some tapas and as the waitress left our table, Marco got to the point. He explained that the emergency in Sudan was really heating up. Two members of the emergency team were down with malaria in a hospital in Khartoum and he was the only available colleague with the necessary experience to step into the situation. I could tell he was all fired-up about the possibility of being back out there and in the thick of things again. He was buzzing and highly charged.

"So," he finished, "I'm due to leave for Sudan in a week and the mission is for three. If I could get out of it, believe me, I would. But there's really nothing I can do." It didn't take me a second to realize the implications for our forthcoming move but before I could get a word out, he looked me straight in the eyes.

"I know I'm asking a lot Kate, but if you want, you could go to Panama as we planned and help set things up, you know, find us a flat, sort out bank accounts – all that stuff. I'd be over just two weeks later. I know it's not ideal, but it would be great if you could. You know that I really wanted us to head out there together but I don't see any sense in you changing your ticket too and honestly, if you do stay back and wait for me, where are you going to stay in London?"

Of course, it had seemed logical at the time. Our lease was up in two weeks and none of my friends had a spare bedroom. Mum and dad were going on one of their yearly cruises and would be half way between Miami and the Bahamas by then. I didn't fancy hanging out at home, alone without them – I'd go stir crazy after day three let alone a few weeks.

"I don't believe this!" I blurted out. "Are you sure you can't get out of it? I mean, they really know their timing!" I was feeling shell shocked; he was finishing off the *Patatas Bravas*.

"I wish, but there's really nothing I can do," he said, taking another mouthful and pushing the empty plate away. "They really need me there right now and I just don't feel like I can let them down."

"Let *them* down, what about *me*!" I could feel my temper getting the better of me. Marco wasn't helping. He seemed more intent on ordering more food from the menu card than on the situation at hand.

"So, I'm supposed to go out there on my own and sort everything out?! I don't even speak Spanish," I said with a sigh.

He suddenly looked disappointed.

"Come on Kate, it's not my fault. I've been on the emergency roster for years and there's hardly anyone else with my experience available right now. You know that it's impossible to time these things and after all, it's not the end of the world. As I said, I'll be over to Panama before you can blink. Look, would it make you feel better if I contact the UN office in Panama tomorrow and tell them what's happened? I'm sure the people in the office out there will give you a hand with everything. Someone can even be at the airport to meet you and help you over the first few days."

For a moment I didn't know what to say. That would surely be better than nothing. Marco studied my face.

"Look, I can see this is a big deal for you Kate," he said sounding slightly annoyed and sitting back in his chair. "But, well, if you feel so uncomfortable about it let's try and find you a place to stay in London for a few weeks. I'm sure we can find something if we ask around and then we can go together when I get back. I just didn't think it was such a big deal. I thought it would be great to get on with things and start getting our new life together sorted out..."

"I understand that Marco, but we were going to go out there together and well... let me think about it. I don't have to decide just now, do I?"

"No, of course not. Sleep on it. Whatever you want to do is fine by me – however you prefer." He smiled. But it was a weak smile and something told me that underneath the smile he was angry, feeling let down. Though it's easy to say in hindsight.

I met up with Melodie the very next day. I'd wanted an emergency session with my friend and she had canceled her lunch date to see me, but by the time I met up with her, I had already simmered down. The late evening news had featured the rising crisis in Sudan and it had suddenly made me feel that maybe I was being selfish. Marco was needed out there. It was a humanitarian emergency. People were dying. Surely, I could cope on my own for a couple of weeks...

Melodie had a different angle, she was looking decidedly uneasy.

"Does he really have to go to Sudan? Like right now? I mean, sorry to be so blunt. I wouldn't normally, but well, shouldn't you come first?"

I returned her gaze and for the first time felt a little irritated. I'd always had the impression that Melodie wasn't a big Marco fan. She'd never said as such. It was just a sensation that I had never been able to shake.

"Melodie, sorry but I don't think you understand what it's like being in Marco's line of work. Sometimes they're really expected to drop everything, sometimes in less than 48 hours – you know when they're on this emergency roster…"

"But what about you? What are you going to do? How will you feel turning up in Panama on your own?" she insisted. "Really Kate. Have you decided?"

"I think I'm going to go on the 4th as planned," I said, taking a sip of coffee which was still a little too hot.

"Are you sure?" she said, looking concerned. A little frown line appearing on her forehead right between her eyes.

"Well of course it's not ideal," I agreed, "But really, I mean, what can I do? I've been thinking about this all morning and maybe Marco's right. Maybe it isn't such a big deal. I'm not saying that it's going to be easy but I'll be OK. He'll put me in touch with some of the people in the office there. They're sure to help out. And after all, he'll be arriving just two weeks later. You know I feel that maybe I should be a bit more supportive of Marco. I don't want to become something else he has to worry about." She was still studying me. I sipped my coffee again.

"Really, I've decided that I'm going and I'll be fine. Hey – do you think they have cappuccino in Panama?"

She laughed, then tried to get the attention of the waiter for the bill.

"Sorry I've got to dash Kate, today's turned into a total nightmare. The editor is coming in and I've got a meeting back at the magazine in 10 minutes. But honestly, I'm worried for you. A new country, new language, new customs, all on your own. Are you really sure you're doing the right thing? And to be frank, I'm worried that Marco is being a bit, well, selfish in this…" She paused for a second.

"Kate, I hope you're not going to go through with this to prove something to him, are you?"

Melodie was very perceptive. In the past I'd told her that Marco had said that he didn't understand how I'd never wanted to live and work abroad and how he sometimes felt that I lived my life through all the books I read, rather than living it myself. Then, just the other day, I had been telling her how Marco sometimes gave me the impression he was a little frustrated with my lack of a sense of adventure. That he felt that I hadn't been excited about Panama and he was worried I wasn't really keen on the idea at all.

"Well, if you want the honest answer, yes. I have been really thinking about things and well, I've decided that I do need to be a bit more adventurous. I've never had this type of opportunity before and well, as you know, change doesn't come easy to me, I'm a creature of habit. But I guess here's my chance to prove to everyone that I'm capable of standing on my own two feet and heading off for a little adventure of my own. It's only a two-week adventure after all and then Marco will arrive."

"Well, I hope you know what you're in for," she said rather seriously, pulling on her coat as she got up to go. "Make sure that you're doing what's best for you, not to prove a point to Marco. And if you change your mind, you can always stay at mine. My sofa is always there for you. It might not be the comfiest sofa in the world but it's got your name on it. I'll give you a call later, OK?"

And with that, she was dashing back to the office, her coat still unbuttoned and flapping as she crossed the road. I watched as she jumped over a puddle of muddy water by the curb and decided to indulge in my second cappuccino of the day.

"Hi Kate! Can we join?" The sound of a voice brings me back to the here-and-now and Panama. In a flash, I see Stuart grinning down at me.

"It looks like rain and I've worked out that yours is the only umbrella big enough around here to shelter all three of us, counting Paco, of course."

Paco, a scruffy, bouncy, honey-colored terrier had to be the cutest and friendliest dog alive. He was positively jumping for joy to see me, very enthusiastic considering we've never actually met before.

"I didn't know you had a dog?"

Stuart laughs.

"No, he's May's, but I often take him for walks. I'm a frustrated dog owner, you know."

"How's things?" I ask Stuart as he grabs himself a chair and ties Paco's lead to it.

"Really busy setting up some new deals but it's going well and I seem to be attracting investors so I shouldn't complain. How about you?"

In spite of the years spent in New York, he still has his Lancashire accent. It's familiar and friendly.

"OK, thanks," I say smiling, taking another sip of beer and leaning over to give Paco a stroke. Stuart studies me.

"You sure? I mean, *really.* How are you settling in? If you don't mind me saying, you did seem a little bit, err, subdued the other night?"

I'm about to respond but Ricky comes over and Stuart is ordering a beer.

"Sorry, so you were saying?" he says once his order is in.

I study Stuart's face. It's a warm, kind face and there's something about this guy from Blackpool that makes me feel more comfortable than I've felt for a long time.

"You asked me how I was settling in and I was about to lie to you," I say.

"Lie?" He looks surprised for a moment.

"Lie, because I was going to say everything's fine, and it isn't. To be perfectly frank, I'm not enjoying Panama much at all," I add with unexpected conviction.

"Oh, I see. Why's that?" he asks with, it seems, genuine interest.

"Oh, well, it's hard to explain, but well, to be honest, I just don't really like it that much."

"Oh, really? What don't you like about it?" he says. He's obviously curious to hear more.

"Well, I'll give you a list if you like!"

He laughs but looks concerned.

"Come on, it's not that bad is it?"

"Well, depends on your point of view of course," I say putting down my beer.

"And what's your point of view?" he asks, leaning forward ever so slightly.

"It's hard to explain…"

"I'm all ears," he persists.

I shift in my chair and I guess he can sense I'm feeling uncomfortable.

"Look, you don't have to talk about it if you don't want to," he says kindly. "I was prying and I shouldn't. I'm terrible for that, can't keep my nose out of other people's business."

"No, I'm sorry. You've caught me on a bad day and at a bad moment. I actually just thought I saw my ex-boyfriend over there and, well, things haven't quite turned out for me here like I was expecting them to. You know, to be honest the problem isn't Panama at all, it's me."

"Ah I see," he says with a knowing nod, taking a longer than average swig from the icy bottle Ricky has just brought over.

"So, there's an ex-boyfriend involved? You didn't mention anything about him the other night. Now I understand. To be honest I didn't really get it the other night, I mean what you were doing here that is."

"Well, I was a bit embarrassed. Jane said I was being stupid, but well, I was dumped pretty badly and it's taken me most of the time I've been here to get over it. And, well, I'm not over it yet actually. Not at all. Anyway, I didn't mention it – you see what happened made me feel like a complete fool and I couldn't bear going into the details the other night over dinner and…"

"Kate, you don't have to explain yourself to me," he says earnestly.

"Anyway, as you can imagine, I'm not experiencing Panama in the best frame of mind, and you know, you're quite right, I'm probably not going to stay in Panama very long, just as long as it takes me to clear my mind and decide what I'm going to do next. You see I was telling the truth about fundraising. I've been doing it now for years and if I hear the words "fundraising", "telethon" and "response rate" ever again I might just go mad."

"And that was the original plan, going back to London and back to fundraising, right?" he asks.

"Yes, you see, it's all I know. After university I just fell into it really – friend of a friend. I went in to do some filing and never left! It was great for a time, easy work and rewarding but it's strange. Being here has forced me to re-evaluate everything: work, where I live, even the way I live my life. You know the furthest I've ever been before coming here is France and Italy. Then London is so expensive. I was just scraping by on my charity job salary. Do I really want to go back to that? To the rat race?"

"Well, maybe you can't see it now Kate, but maybe this is all for the best. Maybe it's good for you to take some time out and re-evaluate things. Maybe this could be the start of something new?" he says with a very positive and enthusiastic tone.

I know what he means. Am I starting to see through this foggy haze of depression, to finally see this experience in a more positive light? Could it be just what I needed? Maybe I'll turn things around and re-invent myself, my life. Who knows where I'll go from here! Then on the other hand I'll probably soon be back on a plane to

London, planning the next charity telethon and having a cappuccino with Melodie. Would that be so bad after all?

"But anyway, what happened? What's this ex-boyfriend called? Sounds like he's got a lot to answer for. Oh sorry, here I go again, prying into things that don't concern me again, I'm sorry…"

"Stuart, don't worry," I say laughing, "It's fine!"

And then I find I'm telling Stuart the whole story. It's a long one. It takes most of the afternoon. And two hours later I thank my lucky stars: for friends like Jane, for bumping into Stuart and for the downpour which opens up above us and clears the air.

5

"All the world's a stage, and all the men and women merely players. They have their exits and their entrances"

Act II, Scene VII, *As You Like It*, William Shakespeare

I discover that Stuart is a great listener. He's in the wrong profession and would have made a great psychotherapist. I also discover that he has been single for over five years, he loves living in Panama, he's a bit of a workaholic (his words, not mine) and also loves a good book. His favorite book of all time is Salman Rushdie's *Midnight's Children*.

But today, we are really talking about me; or rather, I am talking about myself. This impromptu lunchtime counseling session has taken me by surprise – but maybe it's what I needed all along. Not only, Stuart is also horrified to discover that I haven't yet tried the famous Bar Blanca version of the cocktail Electric Lemonade. He puts in an order for two but in true relaxed Panamanian style Ricky forgets the order. He finally brings them out half an hour later by which point I really need it. The bright blue syrupy mixture is refreshing, strong and incredibly cold. For a second, I have to stop talking and take a deep breath as an arctic chill hits my system and shoots straight to my temple. It wouldn't take many of these to get my head spinning, especially in this heat.

With the help of the Electric Lemonade I'm telling Stuart the whole story; from when I met Marco in Geneva to the day Marco showed up in Panama. I'm racing through and I'm soon where Marco has told me he has to go to Sudan – when suddenly there's a loud rumble followed by a breath taking, sky-shearing *crack*. Within seconds, it starts raining again and the square clears – dogs, cats, people, all running to take shelter and escape the rain. Car alarms kick started into life by the sheer volume of the thunder are going off in every direction and the noise is overwhelming.

We are the only two people brave (or silly) enough to weather it out under the umbrella. Paco looks decidedly unhappy about the whole thing and lies down with a disgruntled whimper under Stuart's chair, unhappily it seems resigned to damp fur and wet paws. I don't share Paco's view. I kind of like it. It's the nearest thing to cozy I've experienced in this tropical city and the umbrella suddenly feels like a large, protective, private tent, the smell of freshly damp earth rising around us completing my vivid imagination of a boozy camping trip gone wrong.

I must say I'm surprised. Most men don't care about the details of stories like this, but Stuart wants to know all the finer points and frequently stops me to ask a question, clarify a point and get more depth. I can't help wondering if he might actually be gay. Some of my closest friends back in the office in London are gay and I usually have a pretty good "gay-dar". But with Stuart, I just can't tell. I take another sip of my Electric Lemonade and decide that I could easily manage another and that I should save that question for another day.

I had been in Panama a little over two weeks when Marco finally arrived. I'd taken a taxi and Harry Potter with me to the airport to pass the time and was waiting in arrivals in a state of mild agitation. Marco had gone straight into the field from London

43

and we'd hardly had two words on the satellite phone since he landed in Sudan. Email contact hadn't been much better, either. Part of me understood: the situation would be chaotic out there. The other half was upset and uneasy. It was unlike Marco to be out of touch for more than a day. And I had really been on my own out here in Panama from day one. The UN car had picked me up and deposited me at the non-descript hotel – that had gone according to plan. And I had met an admin support from the office once. She had been largely uninterested in helping – just pointing me in the direction of the local bank and set me up with some real estate agents for finding a place to rent. And that had been about it. I had been flying solo since then. But that wasn't all. In London, days before he had left for Sudan, Marco had gotten increasingly grumpy and stressed. He had been working long hours and seemed more and more distant too. But when I had questioned him, he had given me a cursory hug and told me not to worry. He told me he would be much more relaxed and his old self once he got to Panama.

When his plane finally landed after a two-hour delay in New York, I folded over the page of my book to mark my spot, feeling a wave of excitement. My stomach was churning.

But as soon as I saw him I knew something was wrong. He looked tense and worn and close up, I was convinced he even had a few grey hairs. But it was the expression on his face that really worried me. It was more than just a long-haul flight and over work. I could see that he was anxious. He gave me a weak hug, an unenthusiastic kiss and looked at me hard.

"Kate, it's good to see you, but, well, we've got to talk," he said, turning away suddenly and looking at the floor.

"What on earth is wrong, Marco?" I asked. "Are you okay? You look terrible. Are you ill, what's the matter? Tell me."

He shuffled on his feet.

"Well… a few things have come up. Look, we can talk later." He grabbed his bags, looking at me expectantly.

"Are you here in a cab?"

We were soon outside the terminal building. Marco had a cigarette lit, the smoke struggling to drift in any particular direction in the ever-present humidity. I was sure a storm was on the way. The atmospheric pressure was so heavy that I felt like I might be squashed flat down to the tarmac like a tin-can in a press. The humidity had steamed up my sunglasses on the way out of the arrivals hall and I took them off to clear them while Marco loaded his luggage into the trunk of one of the many dilapidated local taxi cabs. I put my glasses back on and, although he probably couldn't see my eyes through the lenses, he must've guessed what they were saying.

"Just let me get to your hotel, have a shower and a beer, then we can talk properly," he said, throwing the half-finished cigarette down on the tarmac and getting into the taxi, the butt still smoldering by the curb.

The taxi ride seemed like an eternity and Marco spent most of the ride making small talk about his mission to Sudan, up-dating me on inconsequential office politics and the flight. By the time we had arrived at the hotel, I didn't know what to expect or think. Marco certainly wasn't himself. His hand had seemed strangely stiff in mine in the taxi and as we sped along he studied the green suburbs of the city with a distant eye.

After what felt like an eternity, we arrived at the hotel. He had his shower and we were finally sitting in an almost deserted bar by the sea. The threat of another thunderstorm was probably keeping customers away but I didn't mind as the night air was cooler than normal and there was a refreshing light breeze. For a while Marco was silent as he gazed thoughtfully at the view – the Bridge of the Americas seemed to mock us with what should have been a truly romantic setting.

"So, how have you been Kate? How you settling in here?" He asked looking even less at ease, lighting another cigarette. He seemed to be smoking more than I remember. Was he really so nervous, or was it just the after effect of a 14-hour non-smoking flight?

"I'm doing OK Marco, but let's talk about you. Would you mind explaining what's wrong? I feel like there's something you're not telling me. There's obviously something bothering you." My mind had been racing in the taxi. Maybe he had been posted somewhere else and we would have to leave Panama? Maybe he was ill? Maybe he…

"Kate, I've got to talk to you about us, about Panama; about…" He looked away and then down towards his feet under the table… "Well, I'm not sure this whole thing is for the best."

For a moment, I was speechless. I didn't know what he meant. He shifted uneasily in his chair.

"What do you mean exactly…" I pressed him. "What are you talking about? That Panama is for the best? Marco, I don't understand." Ignoring my gaze, he called the waiter over and ordered his second beer. Turning back to me, he went on.

"Kate, being in Sudan in the emergency, well, let's just say that I realized how much I've missed that old way of life, living in the heat of an emergency, getting my hands dirty, being right where the action is. I realized that if I'm over here stuck in yet another office… well, I'll go mad."

"So, you don't want to come to Panama? I don't believe it! Isn't it a bit late for that?" But he wasn't listening and continued.

"You see, I think I was trying to kid myself that being in Panama would be better than somewhere like London. That I'd be closer to the field, but I always knew deep down that there's not much in this region to keep me stimulated to keep me, interested…"

"So, what you're saying," I interrupted, "is that unless you're out there in some god-awful place literally saving lives, handing out blankets, organizing deliveries of supplies, sinking wells, whatever, that it's not happening for you, you're not happy?"

"That's it!" he said looking animated. "That's exactly it. Being out there in Sudan made me realize what I've been missing these last years. I guess I'm just not cut out for shuffling papers around on a desk all day."

"Marco, that's what I'm saying. So, you think we've made a mistake coming to Panama? But I thought you wanted to come here, Marco, I just don't get it!"

"Well, that's the other part of the problem," he said shifting again uneasily in his chair, his thumb playing with the label on the beer bottle. He was gradually working it off, the humidity and damp from the condensation helping his thumb nail scratch it away.

"I guess that being back out in the emergency team made me realize how much I had missed it and that, well, we're very different people. We want different things you and me. You crave comfort, security, to make a base somewhere and to build a home, have a family maybe. Well, I just don't. I don't want to be 'settled-down' you see, Kate, it's not just the office that is suffocating me…"

I was speechless.

"I know that this all probably comes as quite a shock to you," he continued. His tone was measured, slow. I could imagine him practicing this speech on the plane, "but well, it has been on my mind for some time and… well I just don't think it's going to work between you and me. Like I said, we're just too different. I guess for a while I was kidding myself that if we came over here together, things would change, you'd understand me and what I want from life, that you'd change too but…"

"Marco, have you met someone else?" I interrupted. I could tell immediately that he had by the way he looked in the opposite direction. He didn't have to say a word.

"You've met someone else!"

"Kate, I'm so sorry. I wasn't going to tell you, but well, I think that now you've asked maybe I should be completely open and honest with you. I met her in London just before I left for Sudan. Nothing really happened in London. I swear. But well then, she was posted out in Khartoum too, in the same office and… errm… let's just say one thing led to another and er, well, we kind of got together over there."

47

My mind was racing, and for a moment I thought I was going to be sick.

"Who is she?!" I demanded, holding onto the arms of my chair like it was a white-knuckle ride at the fairground and feeling as sick in the stomach too.

"She's called Candice and, well, she works in the emergency team too. She was a doctor. She just joined the UN from *Medicin Sans Frontiers*. She was actually the one who insisted I come over here to see you, to tell you rather than telling you over the phone, and I have to say I think she was right. Believe me, I didn't expect this to happen at all, but given our differences, I think it's for the best – I mean for you too. We wouldn't be happy together Kate. You certainly wouldn't be happy with me – I want to go and live in Africa again and you don't. You would never even consider it and now I've had time to think it through, I don't want to be in Panama."

I decide that I won't go into any further details of the rest of that terrible evening now, with Stuart. I'm not going to tell him how I cried all night, how Marco tried to comfort me but ended up checking out of the hotel that very night. But I think he gets the picture pretty clearly.

I tell Stuart how, over the course of the next few days, I found out some basic information from Marco. It seemed Candice is French. They had met for the first time five years ago when they had been in the field and, at that time, had had a "minor fling" in Angola. Five years later we're no longer talking about a minor fling. Marco told me that they're getting married in October in Paris and are both being posted to the Congo.

Marco left Panama two days after arriving.

The only evidence I had that he had ever been in Panama was the stub of his airplane boarding pass, a half empty packet of French cigarettes on the bedside table… and my broken heart.

By the time I finish the story I'm feeling decidedly tipsy.

"Wow" says Stuart with conviction when I finally finish, putting his glass down with determination.

"That's one of the best stories about being dumped I've ever heard!" As soon as the words are out, he looks abashed.

"Sorry! I didn't mean that; it's just…"

"Don't worry," I say. Stuart's frankness and the cocktails have made me see the funny side of my situation and now we are both laughing loudly across the square. Ricky comes over.

"*Oy, chicas*, what's so funny?" And just one look from me tells Stuart that he had better never, ever tell Ricky what we are laughing about.

"Seriously that's terrible," says Stuart quietly, looking over his shoulder after we stop giggling and Ricky is off serving another customer.

"I can't believe the guy, that Marco. What a nerve! I mean all this stuff about missing the field, you being very different people. Couldn't he have worked that out *before* he asked you to marry him and moved you over here! I tell you, that relationship with Candice won't last."

"Thanks Stuart. You're sweet." I feel like giving him a hug. It's nice for once to get the male perspective and hear that another guy also thinks the whole thing is crazy. And once again, I can't help wondering if Stuart is gay. There's something about his mannerism and the way he commented on Marco's picture when I showed him. He's almost like a girlfriend rather than a guy friend. It actually makes me feel so at ease.

"You know what hurt me the most, was when he implied that I was suffocating him. It was such a knife in the heart. I'd always known we were different, but I thought that we complemented each other, that he loved me for who I was. But when he said that, I knew I had been wrong all the time and that, well, I guess in the end he didn't love me at all." We are quiet for a moment. My head is fuzzy with too many Electric Lemonades.

49

"Well, if you ask me I think the guy is bloody immature!" says Stuart sternly and with real strength of feeling. "You just don't go around asking someone to marry you and then run off to Africa with another woman! If I ever got my hands on him; well, I'd give him a piece of my mind."

And right there and then I know that Stuart is already my very good friend from Blackpool.

6

"Good books, like good friends, are few and chosen; the more select, the more enjoyable."

Louisa May Alcott

The breeze from the sea is a life saver tonight. I'm basking in it. We are all at Nat and Beth's for dinner and everyone is sitting on their large roof top patio. For the first time in months I'm wearing a light weight cardigan and it feels great.

From the terrace there's an uninterrupted view of the modern part of the city. I'm not normally a fan of this modern sky scraper skyline. Half of the buildings are still under construction and have ugly cables and girders poking out. They look like the bones and sinews of modern-day giants about to stride over the bay, but the almost purple night time darkness conceals all these imperfections and right now I have to admit that the view is stunning. For a moment I could almost believe I'm in New York.

Hippy Beth just showed me "the temple". It's a simple room at the back of their flat but I was impressed with how they've transformed it. They covered the walls with images from all religions and there are candles and sandalwood incense burning on a make-shift low-lying altar. If you were into all that kind of stuff it certainly would feel like a haven from the madness we call the real world. There is a beautiful Tibetan painting at the center of the altar and lots of cushions on the floor where people can sit and meditate. I ask her about one painting which captures my attention.

"That's the god Shiva. I picked it up on my last trip to India. We haven't been there for over a year now. I'm planning another trip soon but Nat's business is really picking up and we need to be here right now. Don't you feel the vibe in here, Kate?" she says, taking my hand in hers and softly rubbing it, closing her eyes in concentration. I'm a little freaked but let her continue.

"You really would be most welcome to join on Wednesdays. Meditation is a very good way of clearing the mind of all the negative energy, so you can see the clear path. You know that's how Nat and I ended up here don't you? I was meditating one day in Santa Monica by the sea and had a vision about Nat and I being in Panama, and here we are!"

I decide that, try as I might, this is all far too hippy, tree hugger for me – much as I might need some help with "seeing a clear path" right now. Beth releases my hand kissing me on both cheeks.

"You are a supreme being Kate. Remember that. We are all God's children. Blessings," she says with a serene smile. "Now I must get back to the kitchen and check on the fish."

Slightly relieved to be back in the real world on the terrace I see that Jane is sharing a hammock with Stuart and they're deep in conversation. I can hear little bits and it sounds like Stuart is telling Jane about the property market in Panama again. I smile to myself. Stuart's a really funny, interesting, sensitive guy when he stops talking about property for five minutes. And in spite of the weird hippy stuff, even New-Age Beth and Nat are really growing on me. And I can't help noticing that, all of a sudden, I feel more relaxed and content than I have for such a long time. And one thing is for sure – since my afternoon with Stuart, I'm feeling almost like a different person.

I have been completely open to everyone about why I'm in

Panama and what happened with Marco. Rather than feeling like the fool who's been dumped, I'm finding out just how much people relate to me. Jane had been right. Seems everyone here has a story to tell and I'm realizing that my situation is nothing that special. People are sympathetic, of course, but then the conversation moves on. Not only that, it seems that the people who end up in Panama end up here for even stranger reasons. Jane with her US visa issues, Beth and Nat through mediation, Stuart to set up his fund and make his millions. And then there's me. Nothing out of the ordinary at all it would seem.

"How's the Spanish going?" Nat asks me as he hands me a glass of beautifully chilled white Chardonnay.

I had decided to start a Spanish class last week to pass the time and get me out of the flat and found a small, personal school in a green suburb of the city.

"It's hard," I admit, "but coming along slowly. It's my first week so I'm still on pretty basic stuff. It's a good way to pass the time, though."

"Well, I think it's great," Nat continues taking a sip of his beer. "I've been here a year and I'm still just at beginner level. Actually, my Spanish sucks."

I had heard Nat's Spanish and he certainly isn't a beginner. He's only being modest. May arrives with Paco and gives everyone a hug, Paco bouncing and running around excitedly, happy chappy that he is.

"Oh my god, what a day! Give me a beer *please*, I'll eat later!" she jokes. "Work is crazy at the moment, I have this new boss Franki and he wants everything done, you know, like yesterday! 'Give me that report,' and 'how is that going?' and 'can you print me off 20 copies for my meeting?' Kate you're so lucky. Make the most of taking time out. When you're back in the rat race, you'll be dreaming of days like you've probably had today.

"What you been up to, by the way? How's the Spanish?" She takes a good long sip of beer and sighs.

"Good, but it's hard!" I tell her. "All those verb conjugations."

"Oh, well, stick at it and it will fall into place soon," she says, and then more seriously, when she knows the others aren't listening, whispers discreetly: "How about Marco, has he been in touch? Still no email, nothing?"

I had met May and Jane at the weekend for a coffee and had given May the truncated version of my story too. May couldn't believe it at first and seemed sure that Marco would re-consider and make some big gesture to try and get back together with me. I'm also beginning to suspect that, in the nicest possible way, May is a bit of a gossip. She is definitely a romantic.

"No, and I don't expect to. I'd rather not hear from him at all, to be honest."

"Hey Beth, need a hand?" I shout, wandering over to the kitchen where Beth is preparing the dinner mainly in order to change the subject.

Nat's fishing trip at the weekend had been the predicted big success. He came back with a 40 lb. marlin part of which is now in large steaks baking in the oven. The marlin should be glad to know that he won't be forgotten. He is recorded for posterity in a photo of Nat holding him up. It's now stuck on the freezer door, held in place by a couple of fridge magnets. I look at the fish. He was huge. His head is almost as big as Nat's. I feel guilty for a second and think about becoming a vegetarian but then Beth is obviously such a good cook, and the smells coming out of the oven so mouthwatering, I decide to leave that thought for another day.

"Oh well, Mr. Marlin, you did not die in vain," I say raising my glass to his photo.

"Sure you don't need a hand, Beth?" I ask again going over.

"No thanks Kate. Don't worry. It's all under control."

I realize that Beth is getting the fish out of the oven and it's soon on the table. Everyone is on their feet, crowding round helping themselves to huge marlin steaks and as if that isn't enough, Beth brings a huge bowl of rice out to the table too.

"Wow Beth, this looks so good." We all agree and have a quick toast, first to Nat the fisherman, then to Beth the cook.

"What a team!" shouts Stuart. Even Paco adds his agreement with a bark and a vigorous tail wag.

"Don't think you're getting any, buddy," May warns and for a moment Paco looks decidedly disappointed, sitting down with a whimper and less enthusiastic tail wag.

"So, apart from the Spanish, what else have you been up to?" asks Nat. He's eating quickly and soon helping himself to more rice.

"Not a great deal to be honest," I say, once I've swallowed my mouthful of fish.

"I've been reading a lot," I add after some thought.

"That's your thing, reading, isn't it? Reading, I mean," he asks.

I get the feeling there's more to Nat than fish and lobster. He's understated but very interested in people, in getting to know what makes you tick. It's like you're a puzzle to him and he wants to work you out.

"I guess so," I admit with no problem.

"And where do you get your books? Have you been to that bookshop up on *Calle* 50, Ex-pat Book Shop, I think it's called?"

"I went up there when I first got here but wasn't mad on it to be honest. It was pretty limited – just a couple of shelves in English. Since I've been here I've bought most things on Amazon, but it's not the same."

"How do you mean, not the same? Don't you find everything on Amazon?" asks Stuart who has been listening to our conversation and is now back in the hammock, trying to balance his plate on his lap. "I use it all the time."

"Oh, Amazon is great for somewhere like this, where there are no really good bookshops. But you see for me, part of the fun is browsing, feeling the books in my hands. Book shopping is more than a hobby; it's an important part of my life. And then of course I love second-hand bookshops in particular. I know lots of great ones in London with real personality. If you're lucky you can find first editions, signed copies – you know what I mean. For me it's all about the experience of going to a really good bookshop. It's a serious pastime. My hobby if you like. I do miss that about London."

"And what do you like reading?" asks Beth as she passes rice round. She's a great hostess.

"Well, just about everything to be honest, both fiction and non-fiction. At the moment I've got four books on the go."

"Four! Really, tell me, what you reading right now?" She sounds really curious. The others are listening while they eat.

"At the moment, erm… let's see. Oh, yes that's right, a history book about the Panama Canal *The Path Between the Seas*. Also *Dr. Jekyll and Mr. Hyde* – you should try it. It's a true classic… erm, oh yes, a fiction by Laura Esquivel called *Like Water for Chocolate* and a book called *Creative Visualization*."

I take a bite of the marlin, and for a moment I'm concentrating on the flavors of the fish and trying to work out what Beth has put in the sauce. It's delicious.

"Wow, that's an impressive list. Tell me, what's *Creative Visualization* about?" Stuart asks from the hammock. Again, I notice just how curious he is to know detail. I like his enquiring personality. Or maybe I'm just feeling a little bit flattered that someone can be so interested in me and what I've got to say.

"Oh, you know, I guess, in a nutshell, how you can use positive thinking to change your life and how you can use it in your art. Whatever that art is."

"I wouldn't mind borrowing that from you, if you don't mind," interrupts Beth. "Sounds just up my street!"

"I never get time to read," says May despondently, "especially at work at the moment, with this crazy new boss, I come home exhausted. Just the other night I was in bed trying to read but I kept falling asleep. In the end I just had to give up."

"How long have you been into books?" asks Nat. So I tell them about my grandfather and the Narnia Chronicles. I explain about being a bookworm at school and going to Cambridge to study literature. I've never really told anyone the full story before, except for Marco.

"If this is a real passion of yours," says Stuart, "how come you didn't find a job in some related field like publishing or something?"

"I've asked myself that a hundred times, but like I said the other day, I just fell into fundraising and after a while it felt comfortable and I liked the fact that I was involved in a good cause. Looking back, I think Cambridge kind of put me off for a while, too. I was so surrounded by pretentious literary snobs there that I just wanted to get away from it for a while."

"So how many books have you got?" Nat continues.

"You know, I've never counted but I'd guess over two thousand."

"And they're all here with you in Panama?" he asks.

"Most of them. I put a lot into air-conditioned storage when I got here and haven't got them out yet. My flat isn't that big, you know, and I was worried the humidity might damage them…"

"There you go!" He interrupts looking very pleased with himself. There is a long pause and we are all waiting while he chews and swallows a mouthful.

"There you go, what, Nat?" says Jane. "Come on, spit it out – I mean, what you were about to say, not your fish!"

We all wait patiently while he chews his mouthful and swallows it down. It takes him a while, first he has to fish out a bone, then he has a sip of beer. Finally, he carries on.

"Well it's perfectly clear to me," he says with a huge grin and an empty mouth, finally. "Forget this thing about going back to London. You should stay here in Panama and open a second-hand bookshop!"

7

"Above all, don't lie to yourself."

The Brothers Karamazov, Fyodor Dostoyevsky

I had two hours of Spanish language class this morning and found today's lesson tedious, to be frank. It's the tourist low season here in Panama right now and so far, I had been lucky to have the teacher for myself. But this morning another student joined the class. Dave is from London, too, and has just arrived in Panama to explore opportunities in computing. He's a nice enough guy but there's obviously some kind of attraction going on between him and the teacher and sometimes I feel like they've forgotten I'm even in the room. Every question is directed to him and the teacher, Rosa, grins and flutters her false eyelashes at him like a 16-year-old school girl out on her first date.

Dave spent the first half of the lesson murdering verb conjugations trying to explain what he did last weekend. And while he did, my mind drifted from the lesson back to the conversation at Beth and Nat's.

What Nat had said has been playing on my mind. I've always had a very romantic notion about owning a second-hand bookshop. Sometimes when I was really bored at work, instead of calculating projected income from a fundraising fun run I'd day dream about owning a bookshop.

I can see the shop now. It's full of character with oak shelves and creaking floorboards. A big fluffy Persian cat called Tiramisu keeps me company. There's a tinkling bell above the door, and the smell of fresh coffee wafting across the well-stocked shelves. It's a haven from the hustle and bustle of the modern world. I spend my days organizing the book catalogues, chatting to customers about the latest best sellers and deciding which Ella Fitzgerald CD to put on the stereo. It's cold outside and I'm wearing jeans and a thick chunky-knit jumper. On slower days, I close shop for a break and to pop out for a piece of cake and pot of tea.

I told everyone last night about my bookshop dream. It was the first time I have ever really talked about it with anyone and suddenly the whole group got involved discussing whether it would be possible in *Casco Viejo*.

"You know it would be so great if someone were to do that. There's nothing like that in *Casco Viejo* and we could really do with it," said Jane.

"I can just imagine it," May interrupted. "And there could be a coffee shop in it too!" she said getting excited.

"Of course, it would be great to have a bookshop here, but making money out of it could be difficult," said Stuart sternly. "Making a living out of something like that, you know, it could be tough. You would seriously need to give it some research and thought Kate if you were ever to consider…"

"Hey, look. It's a lovely idea, but there's no way I'm opening up a bookshop here," I say taking a sip of wine.

"Why not?" asks Jane. "You should keep it at least as an option." I love Jane's frank, no nonsense approach to life.

"Jane, I wouldn't know where to start. For one, my Spanish is at beginner level and well, I've never run a business before. It'd be a disaster. Where would I get stock from? How would I employ people? I'd lie awake all night worrying myself stupid about going bankrupt!"

"You'd learn, if you really wanted to," said Nat. "It'd be a steep learning curve and it's not for the faint hearted, but you could do it if you really wanted to. There's certainly a lack of good English language bookshops in Panama and loads of Americans moving down here. When I started my seafood business, I made loads of mistakes but look how well I'm doing now."

"Stop bullying Kate, everyone," Beth said with a smile. "She'll find her way, bookshop or not."

I thought about it more on the way home that night. It was indeed hard to imagine how businesses made money in *Casco Viejo*. For one, the majority of our neighbors were poor Panamanians who were squatting in run-down or near derelict buildings, their rich Panamanian counterparts choosing to live in the new part of the city on the other side of the bay. The places doing great trade were the bars and restaurants. They were heaving most Fridays and Saturdays. But a bookshop? I just couldn't see it making any money. However, Nat had made a good point. Maybe there was a growing niche. More and more foreigners were choosing Panama and *Casco Viejo* as a place to call home. Buildings were slowly being singled out for renovation and the ex-pat community was growing. Hotels were also being restored in the area and Stuart reminded me that just five years before, *Casco* had been a very different place. It was definitely on the upswing, he never failed to remind.

"Kate, what did you do at the weekend?" Rosa finally asks me in Spanish. Seems she's remembered I'm there and even if she looks completely uninterested in my answer I decide to tell her anyway. After all, that's what I'm paying her for.

The rest of the lesson drags by and eventually, we are handed gap-fill exercises for home work. By the time I leave the lesson and the chilled air-conditioned atmosphere of the school, it's midday and I feel like the luckiest person alive when a taxi cruises by within seconds of leaving the building.

"*Mucha calor hoy* (very hot today)," says the taxi driver through peg-like teeth as he swerves dangerously in the traffic to avoid a reckless pedestrian taking his chances crossing the busy road. He smiles another toothy grin, which I catch in the broken glass of his rear-view mirror. I make a mental note never to go to the dentist here, even if permanent tooth decay or even my life is depending on it. The driver is a tiny old man with grey hair and leathery skin. He sits on a huge cushion which I assume helps him see over the steering wheel that he has in a tight grip.

"*Donde?* (Where)," he asks me for a third time.

"*Casco Viejo, per favor,*" I shout, for the fourth time over the passenger seat. He's nodding and I hope this means that he has finally understood where I want to go. On the other hand, he could just be enjoying the rhythm of the salsa music blasting on his crackly car stereo. I resist the urge to ask him to turn it down and wish Panamanians had at some time developed a taste for Chopin. The lead singer in this thumpingly fast song sounds like a salsa Mickey Mouse on acid and would give me a headache if endured for more than 15 minutes.

The traffic is unusually bad, and as we sit in a jam I can't help but notice how this taxi is nearly falling apart. The window doesn't wind down, the suspension is gone, the wing mirrors broken, but I'm soon distracted as the traffic clears and we speed through the suburbs towards the center and it seems to me that I notice for the first time what a colorful place Panama City is when it's not raining. Unusually for this time of year, there isn't a cloud in the sky and the bright transparent blue forms a soothing backdrop to all the luminous bright green vegetation which is thriving thanks to a combination of incredibly rich soil, constant heat and bucket-loads of rain. It makes my indoor house plants in London look like miniatures as I spot the very same varieties at the side of the road only 100 times bigger.

And then, as the traffic slowly winds its way, like a metallic stream of ants, into the more urban, concrete jungle portion of the city I'm hit by the contrasting ugliness of the decrepit '60s and '70s architecture: high rises, crumbling, peeling, rotting – a lot of Panamanians call these run-down buildings home and I decide never to moan about my almost useless ceiling fans ever again.

Back at my apartment later that afternoon with the contrasts of Panama still on my mind, I'm laboriously trying to work through the uninspiring series of Spanish verb gap-fill exercises when my mind goes back again over my conversation with Nat about a bookshop.

I had found out that May is a huge Harry Potter fan, like me, and Beth is a reader, too. She was talking about a Philip Roth book she had recently read. We would have had a really interesting chat about it, only someone else started asking her about the Wednesday Meditation night and she was in her element about that for an hour. I am beginning to think that I should start a book club. I could call it The Panamanian Book Club. Suddenly, my door bell rings and I'm pleased to find Jane is paying me an impromptu visit.

"Just passing and wondered if you fancied coming out for a drink tonight? The usual gang is going out for our friend Jimmy's birthday. You haven't met him but he's really fun, he's Panamanian Chinese."

I fix us two ice cold Cokes and she confesses that she really fancied a break from her latest web-site project and is rather glad I'm in. I'm about to tell her that I'm nearly always in but don't. I can't help feeling pleased, though. It's nice to know she values our friendship and how can I ever thank Jane for the kindness and generosity she has shown me? Through Jane, I've met some great new people and I'm feeling almost human again. I decide to raid my special stash of English goodies and as I open a packet of milk chocolate digestives, we talk about our future plans. It's clear that Jane is quite desperate to get back to the States to be with Chase. She is so focused on that and so positive it will happen, I can't help wishing I were as focused and excited about what's next in store for me. It can't be easy for her either, I reflect. Him being up in Miami and her being stuck in Panama. She is really an inspiration. Suddenly I feel like opening up – talking to her about me, about the creeping doubts in my mind.

"I just can't help feeling a bit flat about going back to London," I sigh, munching on my second biscuit, "I just somehow have this sense that if I go back it will feel like going back to exactly the same old stuff. The only difference is that Marco will be missing. But I don't know what else to do."

"Do you really have to go back to the same job? You said that you were really tired of fundraising the other day. I mean maybe if you did something different in London, you'd feel differently about going back. It would be more like having, well, like a fresh start...?" she suggests.

"Easier said than done," I say, thoughtfully. "You know at 35, it's difficult to completely change careers. Fundraising is the only thing I have experience in. I could re-train into something else, but that takes time and money. You know, I don't think I'm ready to go back to that student lifestyle again and London is so expensive."

"How about something outside London?" she asks, munching on her biscuit.

"Well, yes that could be possible. I've always quite fancied living in York you know. Have you ever been? It's a lovely city, not too big and full of character."

"But what about your passion for books? You know Nat was right the other night. He was saying after you left that it's the one thing you seem to get fired-up about. What about a change of career to publishing or something like that? If you really wanted to I'm sure with your degree you could."

Then she pauses and takes another biscuit off the plate.

"Or, what about this bookshop idea that Nat was going on about the other night?"

"It's a nice idea Jane. It's always been my dream but I don't know if I have the right personality for it. You know, I think in reality having your own business can be quite stressful. I don't know if I'm cut out for it. I'm not really the entrepreneurial type."

"I don't know, Kate. I think you've got exactly the right personality. You're careful, measured, don't rush into things too quickly. You know all about books which is really important. And you have a passion for it. I think you'd be great at setting up and owning your own shop."

"I'll think about it," I tell her, suddenly feeling incredibly flattered by this string of compliments and for a moment experiencing what could be described as a surge of positivity and a "Yes I can" sensation.

"Is it me or is it really hot today," she says, changing the subject and in unison we both glance up at the ceiling fan above us which is moving the air, just ever so slightly but not seemingly in our direction.

"Thank goodness I've got air conditioning," says Jane. "Stuff the environment and the polar ice caps!" With that, she helps herself to a fifth digestive. Not that I'm counting…

That night we all meet up in the local jazz club Jazz Point. Just a 10 minute walk from where I live, a complete gem; dark and atmospheric with open stone walls and a small stage surrounded by little tables and chairs in true jazz club style. The bar staff and waiters are all wearing Panama hats. A reminder that it isn't just any old jazz club, but a Panamanian one.

We haven't been there long when the first band gets up on stage. The place is packed and tonight it's a free-for-all jamming session. Be that as it may, I'm highly impressed – not only by the quality of the acts but also how cheap a round of drinks is compared to some of the clubs I've been to in London.

I'm introduced to Jimmy, who seems like a pretty friendly guy. He looks young and I suddenly feel old next to his baby face and fresh complexion so I'm surprised to hear that it's his 31st birthday. I buy him a huge mojito and we have a toast while a woman with an amazing voice starts up with *Autumn in New York*.

"My family own three Chinese restaurants in the city," Jimmy explains later when we find that we're sitting near enough to have a conversation above the load music. "And I manage one of them. It's called Golden Dragon. Hey – why don't you come sometime? I would make sure you'd get the best Chinese meal of your life. Our dim sum is the best in town too. Hey, how about dim sum this Sunday?"

"Sure, I'd love that! I haven't had dim sum in years," I shout over the trumpet solo.

"Well, you just have to come on Sunday morning and the others too," he says, looking round the table. "Everyone to mine on Sunday for dim sum!"

The next band is soon on the stage and the tempo changes. The saxophonist is an old guy with a long white beard and the worst Hawaiian shirt I've ever seen in my life, but in spite of this loud and crazy shirt the jazz is remarkably smooth and languid and the whole room goes quiet, a welcome break to the incessant chatting.

"*Round Midnight* is always one of my favorite jazz songs," says Stuart leaning over. "Another drink?" he's pointing at my empty glass. As soon as *Round Midnight* is over and the band starts playing a more up-tempo number, the restless crowd is off again, talking, going to the bar, some up dancing. I've never been to such a frenetic jazz club before, but somehow I just love it.

Sunday morning, the sun is shining and the air is clear and fresh. When we arrive at the restaurant, it's packed with Chinese and Panamanians alike. Who would have thought it, but this is obviously the place to be at 10 on a Sunday morning in Panama City. Beth and Nat are busy with their temple on Sundays, but Stuart, May and Jane are all here, eager and with high expectations.

"I've been here loads before Kate, and I can tell you, I just roll out of here every time. Last time I didn't have to eat for a week!"

says Stuart. "Do you remember, May? You said you had to go home and lie down!" We all laugh and I find it hard to imagine May eating so much, she's so petite, so slim.

Before long, Jimmy comes over and shows us through the crowded, chattering tables to a big, empty round table at the back. Before I can blink, the trolleys are coming by and we let Jimmy do all the choosing. The table is soon festooned with little round silver trays with steaming dumplings of all sizes, shapes and colors. It's hard to know exactly where or how to start. The first one I try seems to be some kind of pork with very fluffy dough.

"What do you think?" Jimmy asks through a mouthful of prawn and green tea.

"Wonderful, simply delicious," I say and I really mean it. Who would've thought I'd be eating some of the best dim sum in my life in Panama City on a Sunday morning.

Jimmy is a super-sweet guy. He's only 31 but seems older than his years in many respects, especially considering he's managing this huge restaurant with all the stresses and strains that must entail. I soon find out that he went to school in Chicago which explains his amazing English. He's very open and before long, he's leaning over the table, telling me how he's currently suffering from a broken heart. The girl he wanted to marry ran off with a French guy a year ago and he hasn't seen her since. I can't help laughing. Seems Jimmy and I have more in common than I thought.

The dumplings are mouthwatering. Light, fluffy, just like little clouds, each with a surprise awaiting you at the center. I play a game with myself and try to guess before biting into each one what's going to be inside: pork, shrimp, or vegetables. It's hard to know and I get most of them wrong.

Back at my flat later, feeling stuffed like one of the dumplings I've just devoured and about just as lethargic as one can be, I try to read my latest Marian Keys book but I can't quite seem to settle on the words. I put it down and contemplate the ceiling. There's a damp patch near the window where I think water might be slowly leaking through from the balcony above. For a while I try to remember if I've noticed this before or if I've just spotted it now. Not that it really matters but for some bizarre reason it bothers me that I don't know. I decide to take a shower to cool down, even if for just a few minutes. Getting undressed, I take a look at myself in the bathroom mirror and suddenly realize what a mess I look.

For starters, I have probably put on a good 10 pounds. All this comfort eating and drinking is beginning to show. Then my naturally red hair, touched up by an occasional dye to cover the grey, is really dry and brittle and the grey really beginning to show through. Besides that, I'm looking spotty, sweaty and tired. Enough said. I head for the shower and decide to book an appointment at the hair dressers as a matter of some urgency.

The water is cool and invigorating and, as I feel it washing away the grime and sweat this tropical city forces me to endure every day, I start to contemplate my future, my life, what I'm doing here, and what I should do next. I have to decide. What am I doing with my life? I'm starting to enjoy things here in Panama, surprisingly. But I can't hang out here forever, lunching, going for dim sum and drinking Electric Lemonade cocktails. It's clear, whether I like it or not I have to make some choices and take control of things. It's time to move on.

8

"The love of learning, the sequestered nooks
And all the sweet serenity of books."

Morituri Salutamus, Henry Wadsworth Longfellow

I've booked my ticket home to London. I'm leaving in just over a month on Delta flight DA599 with a week stop-over in New York – a treat to myself, which also gives me the chance to visit a very good, old friend of mine, Patricia.

I met Patricia when I started in fundraising years ago and we really hit it off. She was quite a live wire back then – not the type of person I'd usually bond with overnight but we had a nightmare boss at the time and we found solidarity and friendship through adversity. Then she met Mike, had a whirlwind romance, got married and moved to the States. I've been in touch ever since but have never been to New York, so not only will it be great to see her again after so long but it'll also be a welcome diversion on this trip back home. The trip home – just the thought of it gives me a wave of anxiety and I suddenly feel the need for an Electric Lemonade to calm my nerves.

Bar Blanca is unusually quiet but Ricky is on top form.

"*Hola Chica*, what you want today?"

"How about an Electric Lemonade?" I ask. "Can I have one of those?"

"Sure, of course. Coming right up," he grins back.

I've realized recently that Ricky flirts with everyone. For a moment, I was almost disappointed. I guess it was just nice to have my confidence boosted for a while. But then again, the constant flirting can be annoying, too.

He's on his way back to the bar to put in my order and I notice that he's already caught the eye of a young American girl on the next table who just sat down with some friends. He's soon over to their table with a menu and a big smile. He certainly is charming, I'll give him that.

When the *Electric Lemonade* arrives, looking very blue and luminescent in the late afternoon sunlight, I take a sip and as the lemonade and vodka trickle down my throat like nectar I wonder why I've been drinking beers and not this wonderful refreshing blend for so long.

I think back to the last few weeks and suddenly realize how much better I've been feeling about things – about Marco. At least he's not on my mind 24 hours of the day like before. I have been much more sociable than in a very long time, too. Last week, Jane took me and a friend of hers named Kristy in her beat up four-wheel-drive to some local beaches. Kristy is a brash, fun-loving American. She works in real estate and is not really my type. She spent most of the journey there and back talking about recent dates she has had and men in general, not my favorite topic right now, but we had fun nevertheless and I took my first swim in the Pacific Ocean.

The week before, May invited me to a UN BBQ and the evening was surprisingly entertaining. I had always thought UN types would be boring (except for Marco, of course). Instead, there was even some dancing and at the end I swapped numbers with a couple of women who promised to give me a call next time they're out in *Casco Viejo*.

I take another sip of the Electric Lemonade and find myself reflecting that I probably have more friends here than I have back in London or ever had in my life for that matter.

The other strange thing is that I'm not feeling the heat like I was in the beginning and more than that, I actually quite like it. Growing up Lancashire, the cold is a part of your blood, part of your bones and you grow up with the taste of the freezing wet moorland air in the back of your throat. Don't get me wrong, I've never liked this biting cold winter weather but have always had a fondness for the cozy feel of an evening in by the fire, the local pub at Christmas, hot tea and muffins after a long Sunday afternoon walk.

My mum and dad's house is a small, sandstone cottage just outside Lancaster overlooking the moors at a place called Dolphinholme. It has to be one of the draftiest houses I know. Under doors, between attic timbers, up through the floor boards – the bitter wind finds its way in. Even with central heating, we spent most winter evenings in the back room with a log fire burning, the heavy curtains drawn tight as much for keeping out the drafts as anything else. Bedtimes involved, boiling hot water bottles, bed shocks and a huge duvet with a pink floral pattered cover. It's a million miles away from the tropical heat of Panama and now that my body has adjusted to these excessive temperatures, I find that I'm enjoying it. Winter starts early in Lancashire and here I am in flip-flops, a t-shirt and shorts. It's just another reminder how England seems not just thousands of miles away but another universe away.

That afternoon I had printed off my Delta Airlines booking reference number and put it on the pin board in the kitchen. It hung there wafting slowly in the breeze from the ceiling fan, like it had a life of its own. I stuck another pin in to anchor it down. I don't want it waving at me every day for the next month reminding me of the decision I've made.

I have found a small furnished apartment to rent in Balham, South London. It's amazing how you can organize your whole life online these days. It might not be the best apartment in the world but it will be fine for a start. I also spoke to my ex-boss. Amazingly the person who replaced me left two months back and my post is now vacant again. He was delighted to hear that I'm coming back to London and said that I can have my old job back if I want it. It's all very comfortable and easy. It's all very... me.

Later that evening I'm back in my apartment checking my email and feeling about as flat about things as yesterday's uneaten pancakes. I had thought the decision to go home would leave me feeling excited, relieved, comforted, but it doesn't. It leaves me feeling strangely empty.

I'm scrolling down the page and then suddenly there it is, standing out at me like a big red unwelcome pimple on the end of my nose, an email from Marco. What on earth could he possibly want? My mind races. Has he had a change of heart? Has he realized he's made a big mistake? Is he on the plane right now with a big bunch of roses as we speak desperate to make up? I want to know, yet I just can't bring myself to open the email...

I click off my Hotmail account, check the cinema listings, search for a place to stay in the *San Blas Islands* where Jane and I have decided to take a short break. I check my Amazon account to see where my latest order of books is, and then I busy myself in my bedroom putting my books back into alphabetical listing by author. Finally, I make myself an herbal tea, one tradition I have refused to give up, in spite of the tropical climate, and go back to my laptop.

I click on the box and my first impression is that it's a relatively short email from Marco. Just a line or two. I skim read it and for a moment don't understand what he's saying, and then I grasp it:

Dear Kate,

I hope you are OK and that life is treating you well wherever you are in the world. I imagine you're back in London? I'm writing today to ask you a favor. I would be very grateful if you could send me my suits. I think

71

you should have them as they were in our shipment to Panama. As you know they were Armani and quite expensive. Maybe you remember them as we bought them together in Rome? One is grey and the other is black. You can send them to the UN Office in Congo. The address is at the bottom of this email. Let me know how much the postal cost is and I'll send you a cheque.

Thanks so much,
Take care Kate,
Marco

He has got some nerve.

I write:

Dear Marco

I'm really good. Thanks for asking. I'm afraid I can't send you the suits. When I found them, I threw them into the rubbish along with the other things of yours that I found. But you will be happy to know that they did not go to waste. A couple of hours later while sitting outside at the local café, I noticed a guy. He looked really poor, probably homeless and he was fishing through the rubbish bins. As you can probably imagine he looked particularly delighted to find your suits. In fact, I swear I saw him a few days later wearing the grey one.

Bye,
Kate

I press the send button and sit back to finish my raspberry tea but just that second the phone rings, vibrating across the table. It's Jimmy.

"Hey Kate, how you doin'?"

"Hi Jimmy, just fine thanks and you?" I can hear the sound of the restaurant in the background, the clatter of plates, voices, Chinese mixed with Spanish.

"I hope it's OK to call you. Jane gave me your number. Look, Kate, I don't have much time, the restaurant is really busy but I wondered if you are free tomorrow afternoon?"

"Sure. I have Spanish in the mornings, but I'm free most afternoons, why?"

"There's something I'd like to show you? Can I pick you up around 2pm? Your place is in *Plaza Bolivar*, right?"

"Yes, but what's this about Jimmy?"

"Sorry Kate, I haven't got time to explain now. The head chef is off ill and it's crazy in here. I'll see you tomorrow. OK?"

"Sure, fine, I'll see you then." The phone goes dead, he's gone and I'm left wondering what on earth he's got up his sleeve.

The next day, Jimmy is bang on time and picks me up in his two-seater sports car.

"It's just around the corner," he says as we glide round the square and take a left.

"We could have walked, but I need to get off pretty quickly, I have a meeting with a new potential supplier from China. Mushrooms. The guy imports mushrooms and at a cheaper price than I pay right now."

"What's this all about?" I'm getting increasingly curious. "Come on Jimmy, what are you showing me?"

But before he can answer, he's already pulling up.

"That, over there," he points out of the window and through the rain, which has just started to bounce off his soft top. It's been one of those days, with rain on and off all day.

"What am I supposed to be looking at Jimmy?" I ask leaning forward to see what he's talking about.

"That there. It used to be a restaurant. The only Chinese

restaurant in *Casco Viejo*. It belongs to my uncle. But it hasn't been open in years. He's been ill. Had a stroke. He's OK now, considering, but he just decided to sell it."

"Oh, great! So, you're going to be taking it over and starting up a new restaurant here? That's wonderful!"

"No, no!" he says, laughing. "You don't understand. I've already got enough on my plate. I was thinking about you!"

"Me! Well I'm not going to be opening up a Chinese restaurant Jimmy," I say, beginning to think that Jimmy has lost his mind.

"No, not a restaurant – your bookshop," he grins back.

For a moment I'm lost for words.

"My bookshop!?" I ask in surprise.

"Well, the other day I met with Nat and Beth and they were telling me about your dream. About how you'd always secretly wanted to open up a bookshop. Then I heard that my uncle was selling this place.

"Come on, I have the keys, let's take a look inside. It's been years since I've been in this place. I used to come all the time when I was a kid."

Before I can say anything else, he's jumping out of the car and crossing the road. He soon pulls out a huge bunch of keys and is opening the door. There's nothing to do but follow him.

"But Jimmy, hold on, there's really no point, I just…" He's already inside and not really listening. I can see now why he's good in business and running a restaurant. He's single-minded.

"Well it's much smaller than I remember," he says, looking around. "But it's got potential, I think. Come on Kate, come inside, what do you think?" he says opening the restaurant door wide.

The place is dark and he tries the lights but there's no electricity. It's essentially one large room with elaborate tiled floors and open stone walls. There are three windows letting limited light through – they've been covered over with old newspapers which have long since turned brown and crispy to the touch. I tear a little off one pane of glass and light from the street struggles through the years of grime. It's hard to find any evidence that it used to be a restaurant until we find a door through to a second smaller room.

"Oh yeah, this is where the kitchen used to be. I remember now," Jimmy tells me. "When my uncle closed it down, he sold all the equipment."

In fact, the only things remaining to hint at its previous life are the old white wall tiles, a very big old sink in the corner and rusty old pipes poking out through the wall where I guess the gas supply used to be.

"So, what do you think?" he asks, turning to me. "It smells pretty musty, right? But that can soon be fixed and it could easily be done up. I'm sure I could get you a great price for the place."

"I'm sure you could Jimmy, but you see I've decided to go back to London. I only just booked my ticket the other day. I decided a week or two back but I hadn't mentioned it to anyone. I was going to tell everyone over dinner on Saturday night, once it was all booked and we were all together."

For a moment he looks crestfallen.

"But what about your dream? What about the bookshop?"

"Jimmy, dreams are one thing, reality is another. I'm not a businesswoman. I wouldn't know the first thing about starting a business in Panama."

"Kate, I'm a businessman, I know Panama. The ex-pat community is growing so rapidly. Loads of Americans are moving here every year. Why don't you consider it... I know it's daunting starting a business for the first time but I could help you..."

"Jimmy, I really appreciate your offer of help. I really do but I'm not a businesswoman. It takes a certain type to open up a shop."

I look around and for a moment I can imagine just how wonderful it could be...

"Thanks again though, Jimmy. Thanks for the thought."

"Well, you know what's best for you, Kate. I just thought that if you wanted to open a bookshop this could be the place."

For a moment I see Jimmy is disappointed.

"So, you're leaving Panama? That's a shame." Then his phone rings and he's distracted. When he comes off the phone he looks preoccupied with what must be a fresh problem at the restaurant.

"Sorry Kate, something's come up. I need to dash. Do you want a lift back to *Plaza Bolivar*?"

"No thanks, it's just around the corner. I'll be fine." We're outside now and he's locking the front door.

"I'll see you on Saturday, right? And I won't mention this to the others; you can make the announcement then." He pauses. "You know they'll be really upset about you leaving, don't you? We're like a family here. Bye, Kate."

And with that he's off dashing through the rain to his car. I pull out an umbrella and head back to my flat, thinking about the restaurant and how it could be a wonderful bookshop. For the first time in a long time, I start to cry.

9

*"Yes, I am a dreamer. For a dreamer is one who can only find
his way by moonlight, and his punishment is that he sees the
dawn before the rest of the world."*

The Critic as Artist, Oscar Wilde

I'm lying in the early evening shade in a hammock on the wooden
terrace of our cabana. Jane is on the second hammock and has a long
straw connecting her mouth to a huge fresh passion fruit cocktail.
Intravenous style. I've got rum punch; the sun is setting and, in the
distance, I can hear the sound of waves crashing on the reef. For the
first time, I feel like I'm on holiday and it's wonderful. I'd promised
myself a few days on a tropical island before leaving, and this takes
some beating. It's tiny – you can walk round the whole island in
just over an hour and there's only one hotel which consists of five
individual wooden cabins with dried palm fronds on the roofs. Ours
is on stilts and our bedrooms are right over the sea. It's nothing fancy,
the bedroom and bathroom have exposed light bulbs and the power
which comes from solar panels is intermittent, but that's part of the
charm of being in this wonderfully remote location.

When I suggested the trip, Jane said it came at exactly the right
moment. She'd just finished a project and was desperate for some

time away from her computer. No only, she hasn't seen Chase in weeks – he's been on a month-long training course and hasn't been able to visit in ages.

We caught a tiny 12-seater airplane and as we set off down the runway, the whole thing seemed to vibrate so much I almost expected to see screws and bolts dropping out of the airplane frame as it took off. But moments later, we were skimming effortlessly over the rain forest, which looked like fresh supermarket broccoli stretching off into the distance. Forty minutes later, we popped out of the clouds on the Caribbean coast. The airstrip was right by the ocean and in a matter of minutes we were on the tarmac, dodging the propellers, and our luggage was in a long, narrow boat which had been moored next to the runway. With surprising speed and ease, we were off to our island, skimming over the sea while getting a glimpse of a very different world below; a turquoise world of coral and fish.

The sun was setting as we unpacked in our island hide away with just the sound of the sea and the forest for company. While Jane was still organizing her things, I slipped off to the beach to the left of our cabin and felt the sand between my toes. It felt soft and warm and wonderful.

Breakfast, lunch and evening dinner are all served round a big wooden table in the main lodge house where there are also hammocks and a simple bar. The place is run by a jovial bunch of Dutch guys.

Hans is the owner and takes charge of bookings and cabins. Jon is the cook. He looks like he needs to eat more of what he cooks – he's so skinny his combat shorts look like they are literally hanging off his more-than-skinny behind and I have to resist the urge to run over and pull them up as he moves around, putting bowls of excellently prepared food on the table. Charlie is in charge of day trips to local reefs for snorkeling and serving drinks at the bar in the evenings. I love the bar. It's so simple: made of wood and strapped together with palm leaves and rope. Charlie is proud to tell us that he made it himself and that there isn't a nail in the whole structure. All done using local building techniques.

Apart from that, he makes the best cocktails I have ever had in my life thanks to copious amounts of spirits and fresh tropical fruits. There's something very early-years Johnny Depp about him and for a second, I catch myself flirting with him over the bar, but then reality strikes and I remind myself that he's far too trendy for the likes of me. What I really need is some quiet, reliable, unassuming guy who's going to stick around next time. And Charlie doesn't strike me as the "sticking-around type" at all.

We sign up for a snorkeling trip, and next afternoon he takes us out in one of the dugouts with an outboard motor on the back. We head to one of the neighboring islands where he assures us there's great snorkeling to be had.

I have always had a fear of the sea, so when he drops the anchor – seemingly miles from the nearest island and starts passing around the snorkeling kits – my stomach starts to tie itself up in knots. Jane is like a dolphin and she's over the side and in the water in a matter of minutes, along with Tom and Linda, a middle-aged American couple from Colorado who checked in that morning and joined the excursion at the last minute. I sit in the boat as it bobs up and down, looking down into the sea. It looks so inviting but very, very deep.

"Aren't you coming in?" Charlie asks, pulling on his huge flippers and looking very professional and sexy all at the same time.

"Sure," I say trying to sound confident but feeling less so by the minute. Then Tom, who's already in the water, pops up gasping.

"Oh my god, did you see that reef shark? I nearly stood on it. It's right over there," he says, pointing, and then he's back under the water.

"Err, think I'll give it a miss today Charlie," I say trying to sound nonchalant but not succeeding at all.

"Really? Why's that?" he says while he adjusts his snorkel and mask.

"Let's just say I really don't fancy coming face to face with a shark out there."

"Oh, don't worry about that, it's quite safe. Reef sharks hardly ever attack people." It's a good try but he senses that I'm not going to be persuaded and doesn't persist. He gives me a grin and is over the side of the boat before I can blink.

I try to enjoy the trip back but I seem to have a mild sun burn on my back and everyone is raving about the reef and I feel like I've missed out. Again, my lack of pluck and ability to throw caution to the wind are irritating me.

"See that island over there," indicates Charlie out to the horizon, his almost shoulder length hair blowing in the breeze revealing a small and incredibly sexy silver hoop earring as he steers the dugout nearer for a closer look.

"There's a local legend that says there's buried pirate treasure somewhere on there. From the pirate, Sir Henry Morgan. The story is that he buried his treasure and then murdered all those who helped him so they couldn't betray him. Locals say their ghosts roam the island and can be heard a night, especially when there's a storm. Nobody has ever found it – the treasure, that is – but you never know…" With that, imaginations fired-up, we head back to the lodge the sun already beginning to set over the sea.

At dinner that night Jane is feeling sociable and strikes up a conversation with Tom and Linda, who it seems are the only other two guests in this low-season hideaway. Tom is nice enough and seems quite harmless and we have a chat about what they've been doing in Panama and other holidays they've had in Central America. He's super tall and has thick shiny grey hair. I can't help thinking that he's rather like an aging grizzly bear. He's actually quite nice company.

But Linda is already beginning to annoy me. If I had to describe Linda with one word, it would be brash. Her peroxide hair and deeply tanned skin, which is desperately trying to sweat through her overly caked foundation, is not complemented by her forthright personality. She doesn't seem to listen to what anyone else has got to say and within five minutes, she has interrupted me twice, completely talking right over me. She has an opinion about everyone and everything and really lets you know it. She tells us that they're retiring down to Panama in six months' time after working for many years in art galleries in Colorado. When I ask her what type of gallery, she gives me a curt little smile, "Oh high-end, modern art. Large pieces, generally." She's really irritating the hell out of me now.

The food is delicious, the wine is flowing, Charlie has joined us for dinner and now I'm really enjoying the evening in spite of Linda, until she starts talking about her retirement

"So, we decided to retire to Panama early next year. We've bought an apartment in *Casco Viejo* – that's where you two live, right? Well, it's always been my dream, to open a bookshop so I decided that Panama could be the place. We don't have to make much cash from it. It'll be more like a hobby and I'd hope through the bookshop that we'd get to meet loads of ex-pats like us. I can't wait to get started on it. Tom, did you try the prawns, they're amazing."

For a moment, Linda is distracted but my mind is racing. Linda is going to open a bookshop in *Casco Viejo*?! That was my idea! How dare she! I know that I'm being ridiculous; after all, I'm going back to London soon. So why do I feel so upset by her news? Apart from the fact that she really didn't seem like the book type at all.

"Oh, how wonderful!" exclaims Jane, and then just to make matters worse continues talking.

"We were trying to persuade Kate to do that, weren't we Kate?" I force myself to smile back. "But she decided against and she's moving back to London in a couple of weeks."

"Oh, how interesting," says Linda turning to me and giving me a closer scrutiny.

"Well, I'm sure glad you decided not to stick around, dear, that would be too bad – two bookshops in *Casco Viejo* – I don't think I could cope with competition!" It's meant to be a joke, and we all laugh, but I don't find it funny, not at all.

"Oh, I don't know," Jane babbles on. "A bit of healthy competition wouldn't be bad. Where are you going to have your shop?"

"Well, like I said, it would have to be in *Casco*, but I'm currently looking for a space, to rent or buy if possible." Jane is about to open her mouth, I know what she's going to do. She's going to tell her about Jimmy's uncle's place. I start kicking her frantically under the table. She stares at me, her eyes searching for the answer. I change the subject.

"So, Linda, you must be a bit of a bookworm like me? Where did you study literature?" Something has already told me that Linda isn't a literary type at all, but it's just a snobby guess based purely on the fact that I caught a glimpse of a book that she must be reading on their breakfast table just that morning – a John Grisham.

"Oh, I studied modern American literature at Berkeley," she says, holding my gaze, as if sensing my direction. "You know, Tom and I are constantly at loggerheads about books. I love all types of fiction but I can't get Tom to read anything other than a John Grisham or Len Deighton. For example, I'm currently reading a Hemmingway classic, and I'd love Tom to read it, but he just won't!"

Tom just shrugs.

"My wife's a literature snob – what can I do!!" he laughs.

"Wow, you two have so much in common!" Jane says getting excited and waving her hand back and forward to Linda and me.

"Oh, seems like you could be right!" says Linda and I smile across and somehow know that we just don't.

Back in our hammocks after five passion fruit daiquiris and a little bit more flirting with Charlie, I try to explain to Jane how I feel but she just doesn't understand.

"Why on earth were you kicking me under the table? I was about to tell Linda about the place Jimmy's uncle is selling but I got the impression that's why you were kicking me," she says almost sulkily.

"I'm sorry Jane. I don't know. I just didn't warm to Linda and well, to be honest I just feel a bit funny about her opening a bookshop in *Casco,* especially if she ends up doing it in Jimmy's uncle's place."

"Kate, you're being silly, why should you care if Linda opens a bookshop in Panama? You're leaving for London in a week. And besides, you said you weren't interested."

"I know!" I moan, "I just somehow felt that it was my idea and well, I guess it just feels like I'm missing out all of a sudden."

"Kate, you decided you wanted to go back to London. We've all encouraged you to stick around and open this bookshop, but you decided to leave. How can you feel jealous of Linda and her plans now? I'm really happy to meet Linda and hear about her project. She seemed really nice and we've swapped email addresses and she's going to write to me once they've moved over here and it'll be great for everyone in *Casco Viejo* if she does go ahead with the bookshop."

I can tell that Jane is a little frustrated with me. I can't say I blame her. We are silent for a moment. I'm listening to the waves on the reef.

"Did you really like her?" I ask, almost timidly.

"She's OK; why, didn't you?" Jane responds, her voice coming out of the dark.

"I found her a bit of a know-it-all," I say grudgingly, taking a sip of my cocktail.

"Well, I guess you could say she's opinionated but there's nothing wrong with that. Kate, are you sure you're doing the right thing? You seem so annoyed about her plans; I mean, well, maybe you're making a mistake going back to London? It all seemed to bother you so…"

"It's too late now Jane. I've made my plans and everything is fixed for London, so let's change the subject," I cut in.

I'm feeling unusually sensitive, which is not like me, but thankfully she gets the message loud and clear and changes the subject.

"Now, what about you and Charlie?" she says. "I get the feeling you quite like him and that it could be mutual."

I'm rather flushed by the news that she thinks Charlie quite likes me.

"He's cute," I admit, "I mean, super cute. Did you really think he liked me?"

"I think so! I'll bet that you'll see, tomorrow he'll ask you for your number."

"What's the point, I'm leaving in just over two weeks," I respond. Jane is suddenly silent.

"You know Kate, you've got a very negative personality streak sometimes." She's quiet for another moment. "But I will miss you."

Jane has taken my news worse than all the others. When I announced I was leaving, everyone was shocked and upset. I think they'd imagined that I'd stick around after all. Jimmy included.

We swing in our hammocks. The dark and stillness of the night and the sound of the reef are strangely comforting... and... disconcerting at the same time.

10

"The world is a book, and those who do not travel read only one page."

St. Augustine

It has been one of those overcast days where the clouds make you wonder if you will ever see the sun again. It has been so dark and thunder has been perpetually rumbling in the distance. Rain is on its way, but right now it's of little consequence. I'm at the airport with Stuart, May, Beth, Nat, Paco. Even Jimmy has skipped the restaurant for a couple of hours… and Jane, of course.

I hug each of them one by one. I'm going to really miss this bunch. I'm even going to miss little Paco and he jumps up to me, maybe not understanding that we're saying goodbye.

And I hate goodbyes. What sad places Departure Halls can be. I look around and it seems that in every direction there are friends and families saying goodbye, tears, hugs, waving.

"Next time I'm back in the UK, I'll look you up!" says Stuart with purpose in his voice. Although I know he hasn't been back for three years, so I'm not holding my breath. After all, it's the thought that counts and I know that he will if he does. I turn to May.

"Here are some things for the flight." She gives me a huge

plastic bag full of magazines, chocolate and there's a book in there, too.

"I ordered it on Amazon just for you," she says. "It's called: *1001 Books to Read Before You Die*." It's such a lovely thought that I don't have the heart to tell her I already have it.

Nat and Beth give me big hugs. Nat looks quite emotional and is subdued.

"Have a good trip, Kate," he says. "And look, I don't suppose we can persuade you to change your mind and stay here with us losers. Too late now?"

I laugh, trying to sound light hearted, carefree.

"Too late, but hey – send me some of that fish, will you?" I joke.

Beth is warm and glowing as usual.

"Think positive, meditate and here's a stone I took especially for you from the beach. Put it in your pocket. It'll bring you serenity," she says, pushing something into my hands and giving me a hug, which goes on for so long I don't think she's ever going to let go.

Jimmy looks embarrassed when he gives me a kiss on the cheek. He's a sweetheart.

Then there's Jane. It's hardest saying goodbye to Jane and my eyes well up with hot, salty tears. I see her eyes tear-up too but all she says is: "Speak to you soon." Her voice is choked with emotion. I know we'll stay in touch and that's a big comfort.

"Good luck with the Embassy next week," I say, squeezing both her hands. "When is Chase coming down next? It's such a shame I never got to meet him."

"He'll be here next Monday. Yes, bad timing isn't it? Him being on that stupid training course too. I would've loved for you two to meet." Wiping my eyes on the back of my hand and trying to smile, I squeeze her hand again before picking up my carry-on bag.

"Well, I guess I should get going." I mumble, try to smile and give a weak wave goodbye to them all. I turn away and as I walk to the departure area I take just one look back and they all start waving. Even Paco's tail is forlornly wagging too, his little black eyes pin-pointing me across the expanse of the hall.

Once I'm on the plane, I try to convince myself that I'll soon feel better but I don't. I sit by the window watching Panama disappear into the distance, hot, burning tears welling up in my eyes again.

It wasn't supposed to be like this! I was supposed to feel relieved, ecstatic and excited about going home to London, but I don't. I just feel downright wretched. The feeling doesn't get any better after I've made full use of the drinks trolley. I can see the stewardess is giving me the once over when I ask if I can have a third beer, but I don't care. I give her a good, long, hard look back. She's young and pretty and probably doesn't know the meaning of the words "dumped" and "midlife crisis".

I watch the little computer graphic of the plane on the TV monitors getting further and further away from Panama and every time it does I have an empty feeling in the pit of my stomach and no amount of beer or packets of pretzel snacks is going to fill it.

By the time I arrive in New York, I'm not feeling any better, but Patricia is at the airport to meet me with big smiles and a hearty hug, so I tell myself to put on a brave face and snap out of it. And it's wonderful to see her again. It has been years but we pick up as if we'd just seen each other the week before.

As we walk to her car, I breathe in the air. It's early November and the contrast with Panama couldn't be greater. The cold air against my cheeks actually makes me wince. It's so sharp, so biting. Seems I'm already missing the warm, balmy Panamanian evening air and I can't help wondering what everyone is doing right now, all my friends – it's hard for me to imagine, and it all already seems far from my new reality here. Thank goodness for Patricia.

Patricia married well. Her husband Mike is a New York corporate lawyer and they have an amazing, if small, apartment, in Manhattan close to Gramercy Park. It's very cozy and even has a view down on to the park from the living room. It seems that my timing is good in that Mike is out of town for the week at a conference in Michigan and so Patricia is even happier for my company. We soon settle down in her big, dreamy, cream velvet sofas with a bottle of champagne and two glasses. I can't help wondering how she keeps these sofas so clean. I'd have them covered in coffee and red wine stains within a week.

"The place is just gorgeous," I tell her, looking round and taking it in.

"Wow, I can't remember the last time I had real champagne!" I add, as she pours me a glass of Moët & Chandon.

"We've had this bottle in the fridge for a couple of weeks and this is the perfect excuse to drink it!" she laughs back. "Not that I ever need an excuse to drink champagne!"

"So, tell me all," she says expectantly, settling back into the sofa and taking a sip. "Panama. I want to know everything!"

"How long have you got?" I joke.

"All week! Just start at the beginning and don't miss anything out!"

When I met Patricia, we were both working in a charity in London. It was my first job. I was managing sponsored events and she was in charge of major donors. That's how she met her husband Mike. He was living in London at the time and was a guest at one of Patricia's fundraising gala balls at the Savoy. When their relationship became serious, she left work and moved to the US, picking up work later again once married and with a work permit at an international NGO with head offices in New York. I don't think she works for the salary any longer though. Mike earns enough for the both of them, I think, but more for the sense that she's doing some good in the world. I admire her for that.

Patricia was always going to marry well. She comes from one of those home-counties backgrounds where horse riding and ballet classes as a child are part of your DNA. But in spite of our very different upbringings we'd always hit it off like a couple of "houses on fire" – albeit one, a cottage in Lancashire and the other, a five-bed mansion in Surrey. I study her face and she looks well and her down-to-earth, familiar features make me feel welcome in spite of her sumptuous New York lifestyle.

I give her the basics of what happened with Marco, Panama, my life in London and we polish off the champagne – rather too quickly. It's going straight to my head. Then we head out for dinner.

"I've got the perfect place," she says, locking the front door and calling the very elaborate mirrored lift to take us down to the lobby. "It's just down the road, right on Irvine Place, you'll just love it."

Café Monks is a very stylish, trendy and cozy Spanish bistro-type tapas bar. It's small and busy and so we don't get a table but are lucky to find two spare places right at the bar. The food is varied and mouthwatering and the atmosphere really conducive to intimate conversation. I feel like I've just been beamed down from Planet Panama and I can't help feeling that I'm somehow ever so slightly out of my skin and in a strange "New York limbo-land". I feel lost between two lives and quickly heading in the direction of an old and used-to-be familiar one. There's so much going on in my head that I find it hard to concentrate while Patricia is telling me about how Mike and she are currently trying to start a family.

"It's only been six months, but well, I'm getting a bit worried," she confesses.

"I'm sure it will be fine," I say, dodging my way back into the conversation convincingly sounding like I had been listening to her every word. I give her hand a squeeze and she smiles back and I feel rotten for not concentrating on my friend and giving her the attention she deserves when I've been boring her senseless with the trials and tribulations of my life for the last few hours. She looks unconvinced by my comforting words and takes another mouthful of Brussel sprouts.

"Oh, this is so good. They must've just come in season…"

It strikes me how strange the whole human condition is. It seems everyone I know has some issue they're dealing with: Jane with her US visa problems, Patricia with her desire for a baby, even confident and successful Melodie back in London struggling to find a decent boyfriend suffering one bad blind date after another. This dawning realization makes me feel better and worse, heavy and light all at the same time.

Eventually we've both caught up on the basics of each other's lives and Patricia brings the conversation back to me.

"So Kate, you're heading back to London. I know we talked about it all earlier but I just wanted to say again that I can't say how sorry I am about what happened with Marco. When you wrote to me from Panama I wanted to jump on a plane right there and then. If I hadn't had so much work on, I would have taken some time off and come down to see you."

"That's very kind of you but I would've never expected you to do that! Oh, and I'm fine now," I say, taking a sip from a delicious glass of red wine and wondering why we'd only ordered a glass each instead of a whole bottle. I'm forgetting that Patricia has to go to work the next day and we've already had a whole bottle of Moët.

"I can't say that it's been easy though. I thought the world of Marco, you know. I really thought he was 'The One'. The thing is, going back to London should feel good after what I've been through in Panama, but well, without Marco, it just feels painful and empty, like I'm going back to the same old routine, only this time Marco is missing. I'm trying to see it as a positive thing, you know, like a fresh start, but well, it's hard. I'm beginning to wonder if I should've stayed in Panama after all." The words come out of my mouth and surprise me. "Do I really think I should've stayed in Panama? Now I'm confusing myself." Tears well up in my eyes. I quickly take a sip of wine and force them back down again.

"To do what, though, Kate? Would you be able to get a job out there?"

And then I tell her about my bookshop dream, about Jimmy and his uncle's shop and how – since I saw it – it's been constantly on my mind.

"Look Kate, I've known you for years. You always told me that you regretted the way you just fell into fundraising and never got out of it – I mean, to do something different. And you've always had a passion for books. Maybe you should think a bit more seriously about this opportunity. I mean, it is a really good opportunity, after all. Look, I don't think anyone can advise you. In the end, I think you have to decide for yourself but you know you're welcome to stay at ours as long as you want if you need more time. We'd be happy for you to stay for a while. In fact, Mike has a lot of trips coming up over the next month… it would be nice for me to have the company!"

"Thanks Patricia, that's really sweet but I think my mind is made up, I've got my ticket booked for London next Monday and I'm starting back at my old job there on the Wednesday and well, I guess it'll all work out in the end. But thanks for the offer. I really appreciate it. You're a great friend, Patricia. You know I can't believe that I've never been to visit you in New York before! I'm going to make the most of it!" And to that, we have a toast and throw caution to the wind and I order a bottle of the fabulous Rioja knowing full well that I'm going to drink most of it.

11

"The mind is its own place, and in itself
can make a heaven of hell, a hell of heaven."

Paradise Lost, John Milton

This week is supposed to be about me, about leaving the past behind and moving on, a break before my new life, my new start in London – alone. Let's call it a mid-point, a stepping stone, a neutral space for me to shed the memory of Marco and what happened in Panama and prepare myself for the return home. Yes, I see New York as my turning point. It's supposed to be a bit of fun too.

But in this autumn, chilly limbo land, with Patricia's scarf and jacket to keep me warm, I feel like I'm failing. I can't relax, I can't enjoy it and I'm not fully experiencing the city: the streets, the cafés, bars and shops. My mood is low, my mind distracted and the thought of returning to London next week simply depressing. Was I naïve to think that it would be so easy?

I don't know New York at all and at first, the streets are intimidating. The size and scale of the place, the endless blocks, and the height of the buildings like vast rectangular concrete canyons. Initially, I have an overwhelming confusion about where I am but eventually the grid system and my Google Maps app helps, and before long I've worked out the neighborhood around Gramercy Park and a little beyond. Then I find I'm venturing down to some interesting bookshops in Greenwich Village and soon, confidence growing, I'm off to Lower East Side where my friend Google tells me there are some more.

I'm walking along, arranging the woolen scarf Patricia has lent me so it rests a little higher around my neck to try and keep out the poking fingers of cold, when out of the corner of my eye I see a little side street with some interesting shops and boutiques. My mind jumps to Patricia. It's her birthday the following week and I want to get her something nice and to say thank you for her hospitality.

But thoughts of Patricia's gift soon (selfishly) leave my head as I spot what looks like a scruffy second-hand bookshop. I wander down to take a look and at first it seems closed and I'm disappointed. Shame. It appears the most fascinating place. Even from the outside I can see the books inside piled against the window. They are so far up I can't imagine how any light can get into the shop on even the brightest day. Then I notice that it looks like the light is actually on inside, and I decide to try to be sure. I push the door and it opens – even if it sticks terribly. You have to be a keen book buyer to get in here and I am, so I give it another shove and after struggling a little, I manage to get in and push it closed behind me.

Before I have the chance for my eyes to adjust to the gloom a woman's voice comes over the top of the counter.

"Good afternoon. Let me know if you're looking for something specific."

I look over the pile of books on the counter where I see a woman of around 65, busy sorting through a box of books. She's crouched on the floor and so intent on her task that I don't want to bother her unnecessarily.

"Oh, good afternoon. Thanks, I'm just browsing actually but I'll keep that in mind."

She doesn't seem to be listening but carries on with her job without more than a very quick glance in my direction.

The shop had looked small from outside but I can now see that it's big and a complete warren of rooms and shelves stretching back, branching out like the roots of a large tree. As well as all the books on shelves, there are books piled high and mushrooming out of boxes on the floor in every corner. I can see that categories exist under the chaos but the whole impression is one of almost complete disarray. I look at the shelves near to the door which on first impression seem to house fiction, but mixed in I find history, poetry and a couple of biographies. Dusty books are filling every available space, every nook and every cranny – but what a collection!

Where some order can be gleaned I can see what looks like an entire set of Graham Green. The next room is full of nothing but Penguin Classics. There are two complete rooms of history and I've never seen so many crime novels in one place in my life. The prices are amazing too! Just four or five dollars for a paperback and ten dollars for a hardback. Remembering the pile of books I already have to ship back to London, I try to restrain myself but start browsing. Almost an hour later and clutching a meager (for me) five books, I head for the counter.

"Oh, you found *Heart of Darkness*," she says, going through my selection to add up the total.

She is tall, slender, has thick bobbed grey hair and small red reading glasses. I guess she is or has been a heavy smoker from the deep lines around her mouth and the yellow skin on her right index finger and thumb.

"I really love this book. I must've read it 10 times. I always find it hard parting with a book I like but I've got a lovely copy of this one myself so it would be silly to keep another."

"How long have you had this shop? It's wonderful!" I venture.

"Oh thank you my dear, well, I opened up in, let's see, would be around August two years ago. Did you find everything you wanted?"

"Well actually I'm just browsing today. I'm not looking for anything in particular."

"You're on holiday or living in New York?" she asks looking over the top of her reading glasses and for the first time gives me an understated smile. She has light, but amazingly bright green eyes which seem to have more sparkle than her years.

"Just passing through. I was living in Panama but I'm heading back to London in a few days," I explain.

"Great city, lots of good bookshops." She smiles over before reaching for a carrier bag – an old crumpled Bloomingdales but it doesn't matter.

"Do you mind me asking, how you got into opening up a bookshop? You see I just love books. I studied literature at Cambridge and well, it's always been my dream."

"I used to be a lecturer at Columbia University here in New York, but after 25 years I'd had enough. I was looking for something new to do and my retirement was coming up, then, well I had a huge collection of books at home. It was becoming a nightmare – I didn't have a big enough flat – I was running out of space, so I decided to open up a bookshop."

By now we've moved to sit at a table in a scruffy box of a room where Megan has a tiny office, nothing more really than a kettle, a microwave and a little desk with a computer but I'm fascinated. We're drinking jasmine tea together and she's just opened up a packet of rich chunky chocolate chip cookies. They melt in the mouth and I can't help wondering where Megan puts all the calories eating these. She looks so slim. I'm also wondering how she manages to move around those big boxes of books which are blocking a lot of the aisles. Megan takes another two bites and I wait patiently. She's in no hurry, munching on the cookie and then continues.

"I'd had the idea for a few years and kept looking for a shop, then I heard that this one was for sale. The previous owner had a heart attack poor thing and his wife was selling the business, books and all. So, I jumped at the chance. My flat is just a few blocks from here you see. I'd been left a good inheritance when my mother died so I used that to buy the shop. To be honest, I was pretty lucky with the price I paid for the place. The wife wanted a quick sale. She told me she'd never understood her husband's fascination with the place and was glad to be rid of it. The shop and stock had been neglected when I finally took it over. Infested with mice too! Anyway, I got rid of the mice and added some of my books to the shelves. Even so, I still felt like it needed more, there were a lot of books missing, so I went around New Jersey to garage sales, visited friends, contacts, book buying fairs – wherever, to build up the right kind of stock. As you can see, I probably went a bit too far." She chuckles to herself topping up our mugs with more steaming tea from the pot.

"Can I ask you a personal question?" I ask tentatively.

"Go right ahead my dear," she says munching on a cookie, looking at me intently over the red glasses perched on the end of her nose.

"Do you make a living out of it?" I ask, quickly adding, "Sorry, maybe it's a bit rude to ask you but I'm interested to know how the figures add up. As I said, I've always had a dream of opening up my own shop and it would be great to get some kind of idea as to if I could make a living off this type of business."

"Well, I just about break even or a bit more my dear, although it's early days. As I said, I've only been open to the public for a few years and I'm not well known yet. Anyway, so far it's just been enough to scrape by on but then I don't live a very lavish lifestyle and both this and my flat are paid off, no mortgage no rent. And then when I do have bad weeks, I have what's left of my inheritance as a nice 'comfort blanket' if you know what I mean.

"The frustrating thing is, I know I could do better and make more sales if I organized the shop, did some marketing, you know, but well, I don't have the cash to pay for an assistant right now and nobody works for nothing these days. My problem is that at the moment as much as I try I can't seem to get on top of it. Just yesterday I'd cleared one box of books, then a guy from New Jersey came in with three boxes of books he wanted to get rid of at a really cheap price. I mean, how could I refuse?

"Now, I have another three boxes to catalogue and find space for. It doesn't leave me with any time to start marketing the place..."

She sighs and for a moment looks older than her years – although saying that she hasn't told me how old she is, and I don't ask, having guessed she is around 65. But Megan is right. The only reason I'd persevered in browsing through her shop was the fact that I'm a complete fanatic about books. Many other customers would take one look at the chaos and walk right out again.

While I'm sipping my tea, I suddenly have an idea. I'd felt so at home when I walked into this shop. I glance out through the open door from the office where we are sitting to the front of the shop and feel like the shop is reaching out to me, asking me for help. Megan is struggling to get her third biscuit out of the packet and I suddenly feel real empathy with this woman who is trying to get the shop up and running (for two years now) but is drowning under an ocean of books. An idea comes to me. Maybe Megan and I can work something out, something which would be mutually beneficial...

"Megan, what are you doing tonight?" I ask her directly. I like this woman and something tells me we can be friends. It really isn't like me at all to be so forthright but nevertheless...

"Nothing my dear, why?" she asks over the top of her mug.

"Great! Well, if you don't think I'm being a little too forward, I'd like to invite you to dinner. I have a business proposition I'd like to discuss with you. What do you say?" She looks momentarily surprised, taken aback and then smiles, putting her mug back down.

"OK. Sure, young lady. Who am I to turn down a dinner invitation and your intriguing proposition! I don't suppose you want to tell me now?"

"Certainly not, Megan. Over dinner, which is on me. I insist!"

12

"Beauty surrounds us, but usually we need to be walking in a garden to know it."

The poet Rumi

We meet that night at Union Square and Megan takes me to her favorite French bistro a few blocks south. I can see why she likes the place: small, quiet and personal. The décor is simple, as if it is not trying too hard.

"Madam Beal. A pleasure to see you! It's been a while," the head waiter says, coming over immediately to greet us.

"Oh, hello Philippe. Yes, it has been a long time. I've been rather busy in my shop and I've been too tired to venture out in the evenings. But here I am with this new friend of mine. Let me introduce you to Kate, she's visiting from London."

"The pleasure is mine, Madam Kate," he says, shaking my hand.

"I haven't booked a table, Philippe, but as it was mid-week I assumed you would be able to squeeze us in. Was I wrong?"

The restaurant is almost full, but Philippe leads us to a table after briefly consulting his bookings register. We order a simple dinner of green salad, steaks and a good Bordeaux wine.

"Well, this is nice," says Megan, once we've ordered the wine and start on our salads, which are brought out immediately.

"It's good to get out once in a while. I've been just so busy with the shop and I'm so tired in the evenings that I don't seem to have the energy for much else. And you know I used to have so many friends in New York but over the past few years a lot have been moving out to the country. I guess it's to be expected when you get to my age."

Over the course of the meal I find out that Megan is from New Jersey and had studied at Columbia. She moved on to further studies at Berkeley before moving back to New York many years later as a senior lecturer in contemporary fiction. She met her husband at Columbia, where he was a history professor and they lived all their married life in the Lower East Side. Murray died about five years ago and she doesn't have any children. I realize that this bookshop must be a real focus for her now that she has retired and is alone.

I tell her about my grandfather, my passion for books, Cambridge and my years in fundraising before moving to Panama with Marco. I tell her how I'm heading back to London to pick up with my old fundraising job but have always had a dream that one day I'd have a bookshop. I instantly feel comfortable in her company and trust her judgment although I don't know why. I've nothing really to go on yet at all, only her warm and seeming sincerity although from time to time I get the distinct feeling that behind the warm, subtle smiles she's weighing me up, trying to figure out exactly who I am. Then, I finally get to the point, my proposition. It's surprisingly clear in my mind. I'm not usually so direct and sure of myself – but for once, it feels great.

"Well, Megan, I know that this must all seem quite forward; after all, we only met today and we don't really know each other at all but, well, I'll get to the point.

"You see, we have one thing in common. We both love books and we both had a dream, a dream of opening up a bookshop and well, you're certainly one step ahead of me there! But I can see and you admitted to me that the shop is overwhelming you right now.

Now I'd really like to help you with that. As I said to you, I only planned to be in New York for one week and I'm supposed to be starting a job back in London next Wednesday, but if you agree, I'd like to postpone that by a few weeks to stay on in New York and work for you. To help you sort out the shop. To be honest, I don't see how you could possibly do it on your own and…"

"Kate, that's very thoughtful and I really appreciate the intention but I can't pay you. I don't really have the funds right now and…"

"But I'd like to offer this to you for free. Look at it like this – you get my help and, in the meantime, I learn about managing a bookshop. I can also help you with some marketing. As I said, I'm a fundraiser by profession and, well, that's really all about marketing, a different sort of marketing of course, but the basic principles are the same."

"But Kate, you know that the work is actually quite boring? What would you get out of spending hours sorting out boxes of books and book cataloguing and what about that job back in London. What will your boss say?"

She's right. I'm being quite bold for once, but something is driving me forward. I can call my old boss John in the morning and if he doesn't agree to wait a few weeks for me, I'll just find another job in another charity. There are no shortages of charity jobs in London, that's one thing I'm more than sure about.

"Don't worry about that, Megan. I can sort that out easily. Look, I don't know quite how to explain this but I feel like I was supposed to come across your shop and spend some time there. I don't know why, I have never been a believer in destiny or anything but well, it just feels right somehow. I don't know if I'll ever open up a bookshop of my own, but if I spend some time in yours, then maybe it will finally clear my mind on the matter – once and for all. Hopefully I'll finally get this bookshop thing out of my system or the opposite – I'll decide that it really is the thing for me."

Megan looks thoughtful, taking a sip of wine, she's thinking.

"Kate, I don't know you at all," she finally says. "Some people would say I'd be mad, letting a complete stranger into my shop with no references, but I'll be honest. I like you Kate. I think that you're a good person, and I'm a pretty good judge of character and something tells me that we'd work well together.

"And let's be frank, I could certainly do with the help." She pauses for a second, and takes a bite at the Tarte Tatin which is half eaten on her plate. I sit patiently and listen to the subdued chatter from the surrounding tables.

"I accept your offer!" She looks up and smiles. "That's if you're sure Kate. I mean I don't want to accept unless this really isn't going to cause you a problem back in London?"

"No worries Meg," I say as we clink glasses across the table. "So, when shall I start?"

13

"Books are the quietest and most constant friends; they are the most accessible and wisest of counselors, and the most patient teachers."

The Happy Life, Charles W. Eliot

It's very early morning and even now the city is alive, buzzing with energy and movement. I have a large mocha coffee and two bagels in a brown bag, I'm on my way to Megan's shop and I haven't felt so happy in a very long time. The sun is peeking out from behind some rather ominous clouds and I'm just a few blocks from the bookshop so should be able to get there before there's a shower.

I know I'm going to spend most of the next few weeks sorting out boxes of books and organizing shelves – but that's fine with me. It will be wonderful to be surrounded by this literary mayhem and play a part in the process of putting order back from the chaos. In fact, the more I think about it now, the more it seems almost a metaphor for my mind. In reality, it's just what the doctor ordered.

Patricia was fine when I asked if I could stay on an extra few weeks and my boss back in London John, a little concerned to begin with, took it well in the end.

"To be honest, I thought that you were calling up to say you had completely changed your mind and weren't coming at all," he said with a relieved sigh. "Look, Kate, if you want to start a bit later, I guess that's fine with me. As it happens I'm traveling a lot over the next few weeks and it would be better if I were here when you start. There are a few new members of staff and we need a planning meeting all together before we finalize next year's plan. So, no worries. I'll put you through to Human Resources now, if you can hold the line. You can give them the details. Tell them that I've agreed to your new start date and I'll speak to them personally later."

After fixing the dates with the new HR assistant, I put the phone down with a huge sense of relief. Things were going just according to plan. I felt elated.

"The first thing we need to do is get this door fixed," I tell Megan as I come into the shop, pushing the door harder than ever to get in. It seems the damp air of the last few days has swollen the wood even more. I fight with it to even push it closed and after a short struggle, it bangs shut. "Otherwise, customers won't even be able to get in let alone get out again." Megan is making a cup of coffee in the tiny back office.

"Oh, just give it a kick, Kate! And there are some tools in a box in here." She shouts over while she stirs in her three sugars, obviously assuming that I'm a bit of a handywoman. I think I'll have to tell her later that it's too big a job for me. That door needs taking right off its hinges to be sanded down underneath or it will never stop sticking. We sit down in the back office to have our coffee and I produce an extra bagel with cream cheese for Megan. It starts raining and for a second, I'm overwhelmed by the coziness of it all. After we've slowly munched our way through the bagels, Megan opens shop and I ask what she wants me to do.

"Good question!" she says, peering over the top of her glasses and scratching her head. Her mop of grey hair falls forward to obscure her vision and she pushes it behind her ears.

"There are so many books to organize, it's a bit daunting isn't it?"

"Well, how about if I make a start on that huge box over there," I venture. "It looks mainly like classic fiction."

"That's a good idea. It's been blocking that aisle for weeks. What I do is take out a handful of books and log them onto the computer – come over and I'll show you." Luckily, Megan has a computer and she has already installed a pretty good, basic database so she shows me how it works, how to do a search, enter a book by title, author, and edition, how much she paid for it and how much she has now priced the book.

"For example, Kate, for this box of books, I paid $25 for the lot, so let's see… if you count the number of books in the box and divide the total number by the $25… 10, 15, 20, 25, 30, 40… OK, 50 books in total. I guess each book cost me around 50 cents, more or less. It's a pretty easy method and not perfect but it's the best I can do right now."

I soon get the hang of the database, but I have to admit that it's painstakingly slow work logging each book with all the correct information. It takes me about five minutes for each book which doesn't take me long to work out that I'll only be logging just over 10 books per hour. I begin to wonder how Megan would've managed this on her own.

However, once I get used to the program I pick up some speed and eventually, I am logging on a book every couple of minutes. Once the books are logged on, I pass them in a pile to Megan and she finds a spot for them on the shelves. It takes her quite a while as firstly, there isn't much space left on the shelves and secondly, each category is a bit confused but we agree to tackle that problem at the next stage.

By mid-morning, we are losing some of our initial steam so I put some classical music on Megan's battered old stereo and make our second cup of coffee which goes rather nicely with Megan's never-ending supply of double chocolate chip cookies. It's 11.30 and the morning's just flying by. It's silly but I only just now realize that so far, Megan hasn't had one customer all morning. I ask her if this is normal and she tells me that this is in fact a very slow morning which she puts down partly to the terrible weather. I peer out of the shop door and see that it is in fact raining hard against the glass. "Time to get the door sorted," I say. I put down the pile of books I'm sorting and pull out my phone.

"What you looking for?" asks Megan, "Maybe I can help?"

"We really need to fix that front door so I'm looking for a local carpenter. You don't happen to know anyone do you?" and just then I can see a middle-aged man outside under the awning drying himself off and closing his umbrella. Within a second, he's pushing at the door from the outside trying to get into the shop.

"See my point, Megan. That door is getting worse with this damp weather!" I go over and give the man a hand by pulling from the inside.

"Sorry, I didn't realize you were closed," he says, about to walk away. But I tell him that we are, in fact, open and he comes in, happy to escape the driving rain. We leave him to browse and after what seems like an hour later, he's back, beaming and happy with four books.

"What a wonderful shop you have here!" he says, putting his chosen books on the counter. "I go to a lot of second-hand shops but I've never seen anything quite like this. Took me a while to find what I wanted, but your modern American fiction section is fabulous."

"Well, thank you," says Megan. "I used to teach at Columbia and taught a course on modern American writing. It was very popular." The next second the two of them are off on a detailed debate about Roth and Auster – it's fascinating to just sit sorting books and listen in.

After the gentleman leaves, I start on the next box of books and find a real mixture of modern classics, history and biography. I'd like to buy half of these for myself but I know that's not what I'm here for and resist the temptation to ask Megan if I can put a couple aside for myself. Then before I know what's happened to the time, it's the end of the first day and I'm exhausted but happy and I'm sure that I can see some progress, too. We've already cleared the entrance to the shop which had previously housed four large boxes of books which I'd nearly walked into when I'd first discovered the shop.

"Megan, what do you think about clearing all those books piled up in the window? I could start on it tomorrow?" I ask as I'm pulling on my coat to leave. It's really quite cold inside the shop now. I can feel a draft coming from somewhere and I'm beginning to think that I need to stop off somewhere on the way home to do some late-night shopping for a couple more jumpers – let alone thermal undies.

"… Just that I think it would be lovely in here if you got some more light into the place and those books are blocking it all off."

"Oh yes, that would be just great," says Megan, taking a sip at what must be her tenth cup of herbal tea of the day.

"Kate, thank you so much for your help today," she says, coming over and giving me a huge hug, tea still in one hand and at risk of spilling it. "We've done so much I can hardly believe it! It would've taken me all week to do that on my own."

"I've had a great day and well, I feel right at home, just like I kind of knew I always would." I wrap my borrowed scarf tight around my neck. "Thanks Megan. Have a lovely evening, see you tomorrow morning."

As I leave the shop and push hard on the door to close it behind me, I can't help feeling like things are going just fine. Now, I need to go shopping for something warm to wear… with the temperature dropping, I'm going to need it.

14

"A room without books is like a body without a soul"

Cicero

I've been at the shop just over a week and it's beginning to look like a different place. All the boxes have been cleared out and we've somehow found room for all the books on the shelves. This has been quite a hard task but we managed it by removing the many double and triple copies of the same book and putting them into storage at the back of the shop. It's a sign that Megan painfully needs to improve her system of book buying to avoid all these double and triple copies.

Now that all the new books have been logged on the system, we're beginning to work our way through the various categories and find each book its rightful home. Books are somehow uncomfortably sitting in the wrong places – Jane Austin's *Emma* is rubbing shoulders with *Slaughterhouse-Five*; *Moby-Dick* is back to back with *Memoirs of a Geisha*. It's more than I can bear to see this literary mayhem but today I have another job, I'm clearing the window of books. I'd meant to do it much sooner than now but then a seller came into the shop with four boxes of books and over her better judgment Megan bought the lot, so it took us a few more days to get all those onto the system. Megan seems to buy more books than she sells and I'm beginning to wonder if she needs to make any money out of this shop at all or if it's actually just a hobby.

I tackle the window with relish. The books are rather precariously piled from top to bottom, the only reason they haven't toppled over before now is because the last book on the pile is wedged in and manages to jam the whole lot in place. The downside is that hardly a chink of light is getting through from the outside world making this a dim, cavernous den of a shop.

It's a delicate job. I've already had one avalanche and would prefer to avoid another and the chaos which ensues especially as we currently have a couple of customers chatting to Megan at the counter. As I remove the books one by one and give them a dusting down with my cloth, I can't help feeling like some modern-day explorer who's discovered a forgotten Egyptian tomb. Book by book, as if brick by brick, the shop slowly brightens. A small shaft of light soon crosses the room from the top of the window and reaches the higher shelves of what's going to be the modern classics section at the back of the room. I can see particles of dust slowly bobbing in the beam. There's a lot of dust blowing around and now I can see it I understand why I've just had a sneezing fit. Must be a dust allergy.

The journey down the piles of books continues to be interesting as I uncover all kinds of gems – poetry, literature and a whole section of Shakespeare's plays. I stop for a moment to savor a few scenes from *Hamlet*. I used to know this book almost by heart and it has been a favorite of mine since I studied it for my "A" levels with Mr. Dale.

Mr. Dale was the most dynamic teacher I had ever had. He seemed very young at the time and was wildly enthusiastic about literature, especially Shakespeare. Most of the female students fancied him and word always quickly went around when he came in wearing his very trendy, tight, black jeans. He enjoyed holding additional readings of Shakespeare's plays for his "A" level students at lunchtimes. It wasn't a drama class but readings beautifully voiced by Mr. Dale and not so beautifully by volunteer students.

I can see myself at the back of the room. It's lunchtime and I'm balancing my Tupperware lunch box on my knees quietly listening to Mr. Dale reading Othello. *I'm working through my sandwich, apple and salt and vinegar crisps. Mum is a creature of habit and the only variety I ever get in these lunches is the occasional packet of cheese and onion crisps over salt and vinegar. But I'm happy soaking up the words, the characters, and the plot.*

What is it about literature which has always fascinated me so much? As I dust off the next two books, right there and then, it seems clear: It's surely the possibility each book offers – to enter into an entirely different world whether it's the fantasy land of *The Lord of the Rings*, which I'm holding in my right hand, or my familiar North of England with the *Oranges Are Not The Only Fruit* in my left. To me, every book represents a tiny *Alice in Wonderland*-type door, waiting for me to step through and explore the world in its pages. Maybe lovers of fiction enjoy living these fantasy lives more than living their own? Dusting off those books I start wondering: Am I living through the literature I read? Do I live my own life to the full? Am I escaping into my books and not making things happen for me in the real world? Marco used to say this – maybe he was right? In this moment, I'm not sure what to think, but one thing has become clearer and clearer with each passing day: I'm loving being in this shop and dreading going back to London to a world of fundraising telethons, telemarketing and targets.

I suddenly feel so heavy with the thought of it. And then there's Panama. Even while I enjoy my time in this shop, I've found I'm missing it and my friends there more and more each day. Where have I ever had such a large group of supportive friends before? They quickly became like a second family. I've always felt alone, was an only child, I never had sisters or brothers and I'm beginning to realize how these friends are the closest I'm likely to get.

Then my mind jumps to Jimmy and his uncle's restaurant. I start imagining how it would look with floor-to-ceiling bookshelves, a cozy armchair in the corner, some tables in the center with best buys and latest additions. I go over the figures in my mind – what Megan is making per book, how many I'd have to sell each week, the potential costs. I try to add it all up but it's hard in my head. I don't have all the figures and maths has never been my strong point. I'd have to sit down with a calculator and work it all out. But... maybe it could work, maybe I could make a living out of it after all. And when I reflect back, I wasn't earning much in London. I was really just scraping by on my low-paid charity job... and without Marco's salary, it'll be tougher too paying all those monthly bills.

I dust the last book on the pile and suddenly feel a tingling wave of excitement. Maybe, just maybe...

On my way back to Gramercy Park and with this cocktail of thoughts mixing in my head, I decide to stop in a bar which I'd spotted the week before. The Gramercy Bar is just a block or two from Patricia's apartment and seems to me the closest to a London pub – my old favorite the Blue Flag in Covent Garden – that I've come across in New York.

Patricia and Mike are out having dinner with Mike's business partners but I'm just fine with my own company, sitting on a stool at the bar with my beer, soaking up the New York atmosphere. The bar is old style, with wooden fittings, corniced ceiling and bags of character.

The barman introduces himself as Pete and asks where I'm from. He's a good barman and notices exactly when my glass is getting empty and offers me another. Without thinking too long, I smile a yes, and pull out the book I'm reading – the latest Paul Auster novel.

I try to focus on the words, but it's no use. I just can't concentrate.

I don't know if it's the lively atmosphere in the bar, or the fact that my mind keeps going back to thoughts from earlier today.

I have to start being seriously honest with myself. I've been dreading the prospect of going back to the same old stuff in London and the dread is getting worse. Spending time in Megan's bookshop has made me realize what I've known for a long time – A bookshop is where I want to be: Surrounded by hardback, paperback, biography, fiction, faction, sci-fi, history, horror, self-help, crime, thrillers – the lot.

A chilled gust of November air rushes into the bar as the door swings open and more jovial customers mingle in, hardly visible under their scarves and woolen hats pulled close to keep warm. Wall Street types in suits and ties. I shiver and think back to the balmy tropical nights spent at Bar Blanca in *Plaza Bolivar*.

Taking a sip of the tepid American ale I suddenly feel even more despondent. What am I doing? Why am I going back to London? I see more clearly now that all that emotion at the airport – it wasn't just because I was saying goodbye to my friends but also to the life that I could have built there, of a wasted opportunity, only as usual I'd taken the easy option by running home to London, back even to the same job! Now I feel insanely pathetic and angry with myself and ready for another beer. I'm about to order my third but changing my mind, call over the barman Pete and ask him if they do cocktails.

"Sure! What do you want? A margarita, Long Island Iced Tea, Manhattan?"

"Well, it's not such a common cocktail," I tell him suddenly feeling less shy – the beer is already having an effect. I'm feeling chattier by the minute.

"OK, tell me what's in it and I'll do my best," he smiles back. "I'm not a cocktail specialist. We mainly do beer here but we aim to please."

Within minutes, he's mixing me an Electric Lemonade. When it comes over I take a sip and the taste takes me right back to *Casco*

Viejo. It's strange to be drinking it here in New York with the cold air blowing in through the door every five minutes.

"That's just great," I say taking another sip. "Mmm, perfect, in fact! You seem to have got exactly the right amount of vodka," I grin back over the bar.

"Really? And what's it called again?"

"Electric Lemonade," I say, taking another taste through the straw.

"And where did you find it? As I said, I'm no mixologist. I only know a few of the very popular cocktails."

"Panama, it's where I used to live; well, until a few weeks ago," I tell him.

"Panama. Panama City in Florida?" he asks.

"No, the real Panama – I mean in Central America." I smile back.

"Wow. That's exotic." He grins. "And what made you leave? I mean, come back to this freezing weather? You're English, right?"

"Good question," I say, suddenly feeling glum again. "I've just been asking myself the very same thing, and yes I'm English."

"Sounds like an interesting story…" he says, pouring a glass of wine for a new customer at the bar. His gaze is friendly and intrigued as he hands over the wine and then turns back to me.

I sometimes wonder what it must be like to be a barman. They must see it all: happy people, sad people, drunks; desperate, bored and lonely people… I don't think I fit into any of these categories – I'm the confused and fed-up category, but then as I said, he's probably seen it all.

"Ever been to Panama?" I ask.

"Can't say that I have," he says. "You said that's Central America, right? Hey wait a minute. Didn't we help them build the canal?"

"Sure did, and like I said, that's where I came across this wonderful cocktail. There's a bar on a square where I used to live. It's called Bar Blanca – don't ask me why – and there's a barman called Ricky – it's his signature cocktail." I sound like I'm reminiscing now.

"So, you're living in New York now?" he asks while drying a glass – he's got a dishwasher full to work through.

There's suddenly a cheer from a table behind me. Glancing around I can see that they're watching the baseball game on the TV screen behind the counter. Seems that their team is winning.

"No, just passing through to London, I'm afraid," I say with a resigned tone and wishing I, too, had something to cheer about right now.

"Now that's a shame," he says, smiling over. "I thought you might become a regular."

I go beetroot and fix on the Electric Lemonade. I see that he's made it with crushed ice – it works pretty well – I should tell Ricky, if I ever see him again that is.

"Why London?" he asks turning around and looking up as he fills the glass washer again with another load of dirty glasses.

"Well, I didn't know what else to do at the time, but now I'm beginning to regret it. I have a job there waiting for me you know and I guess it was just easy to go back and pick up from where I left off. Oh, I don't suppose I'm making much sense – I moved to Panama with an ex but, well, it didn't work out."

"So now you're missing Panama and don't want to go back to London?" he asks very directly.

"I guess if you put it in a nut shell yes, it does look that way. I've been feeling a bit, well, unsure about everything for a while. You see I'm in Fundraising – for a charity – but I haven't enjoyed it in years but I guess it's all just coming into focus right now."

I can't help noticing that Pete is actually quite cute. About my height with a slight Roman nose and blue eyes. He's got a lovely smile and thick dark hair with just a touch of grey at the side. He's wearing small dark brown glasses and they give him a slightly studious look.

The bar is quieter now. A lot of people have left or are leaving and it's getting quite late. There are two middle-aged businessmen next to me who are slowly finishing their beers with heads turned up to the TV behind the bar also fixed on the baseball match. After a while the game finishes and they give Pete a nod, up and leave. It's a week night so I guess a lot of people have an early start in the morning. The city that never sleeps – I'm obviously not in the right place for an all-night party, not that I'm in the mood for one in any case.

As Pete is cleaning up behind the bar we chat about this and that and then he tells me that the bar job is temporary – he hopes. He does other work – freelance writing and his dream is actually to be a published author – and he's currently trying to get his first novel published.

"Wow, that's impressive!" I tell him suddenly getting more interested and draining the bottom of my cocktail glass.

"Another?" he asks.

"OK, one for the road, thanks. So, tell me about your book. What's it about?" I'm beginning to feel decidedly tipsy but somehow manage to concentrate on his words.

"Well, look. Like I said, I still haven't got it published… but I managed to find an agent which is a huge deal," he says leaning on the bar. "It's so tough you know. The publishing business – it's so competitive and I'm currently going through a crisis of confidence. Getting an agent was awesome, but then he wasn't able to get any interest from any publishers – not yet anyway. To be honest I'm now beginning to wonder if I'm any good. I did a writing course but, you know, apart from learning a few techniques I think you've either got it or not, if you know what I mean."

Pete tells me that he moved to New York from Phoenix a year ago, where he studied literature, in order to try and get the publishing deal and more writing work. He explains that the bar work brings in much needed cash. He goes on to say that he's always loved crime novels most and has created an Italian-American detective called Frankie Nero.

"You'd be amazed what you pick up in a bar," he adds looking around. "I'm getting lots of ideas for my next book – chatting to

114

customers, overhearing conversations. That is, when I'm not behind here just washing glasses," he says with a wry smile as he unloads the second batch of glasses from the glass washing machine.

"Well, I think it's wonderful. I really admire you for trying," I say and I really mean it.

There's something about this guy I really like. He's easy company and before long I find myself telling him about my life in Panama, the bookshop here in New York, Megan, how I'm beginning to wonder if going back to Fundraising is a huge mistake. Another few sips later I'm even telling him about my dream to open up a bookshop, how Nat had suggested I do it in Panama and I finish the story with when Jimmy showed me his uncle's restaurant.

"So, you think that's what you'll do, in Panama? Sounds exciting. Do you have any experience in business?" he says sounding interested. It's an innocent question but I come back to reality with a bump.

"No, I don't. In fact, I'm not that practical, and terrible with numbers. Oh, who am I kidding? I'm never going to change all my plans, give up a good, secure 9–5 job in London and head back to Panama for this hair-brained idea." I suddenly feel like such a fool. "Sorry, I shouldn't be boring you with all this. It's the cocktail talking… it was the Electric Lemonade that got me started off…"

"No worries, part of my job," he says grinning. "I've become a great ear since working here. And hey, I think the bookshop's a great idea. You could even stock my book once I'm famous, you know, big like Elmore Leonard or someone. I'll even come down and do a book signing for you, how's that?" he jokes kindly.

The bar is closing shortly and, in spite of Pete being super nice about my ramblings, I'm feeling deflated all over again. Then suddenly, in a haze, we're swapping telephone numbers and he promises to pass by the bookshop before I leave.

It's been a strange roller coaster of a day, but at least it's ending on a high note.

"You know it was fun meeting you," he says leaning on the

bar and looking still quite fresh after what must've been a busy long shift. "I haven't met many people since moving to New York who I can talk to about books, writing, and publishing. I joined a course but gave it up – far too high brow for me. They kind of looked down on me for writing detective novels. You going to be OK getting home?" he says, looking concerned as I lose my footing for a second and wobble inelegantly off my bar stool. I'm suddenly feeling quite tipsy and probably shouldn't have had all those beers and cocktails on an empty stomach. It's not like me at all. I'm usually very sensible about this type of thing. I totter to the door, trying not to sway too much.

"I'm fine, thanks. No problem."

"Goodnight Kate! Great to meet you and, if you need another Electric Lemonade, I'm here most nights except Wednesdays and Thursday – my nights off."

"I might just take you up on that!" I say trying to focus on him. I'm not quite seeing double but almost.

I head out into the cold night air and off in the general direction of Gramercy Park. The air is freezing now and it slaps my face hard, on the cheeks. My mind clears a little and I'm grateful that Patricia's place is just around the corner. Somehow, I get into the lobby but have to ask the doorman which floor Patricia lives on – I just can't remember. As soon as I get in I head for the kitchen and fix myself a huge, inelegant cheese sandwich. Patricia and Mike are still out and in spite of my better judgment (I know I'm going to get crumbs everywhere) I take the sandwich and glass of milk to bed. Once in my room I switch on the TV and demolish the sandwich. My mind is so hazy, and most of the conversation with Pete is already a bit of a blur, but I find his telephone number in my jeans pocket on the back of a beer mat and put it on the side then fall asleep on the bed.

The alarm rings and I wake up with a start. The breakfast news is on and I feel uncomfortable in my jeans. Damn, I must've slept like this all night. Stumbling into the bathroom I see through blurry eyes and a pounding headache that I also completely forgot to take off my make-up the night before. It's now halfway down my face. Seems those Electric Lemonade cocktails are pretty strong, after all. I take a couple of aspirin and the conversation with Pete comes rushing back. For a second, I'm mortified. He must think I'm a complete fool, blabbering on about a bookshop in Panama when it's obvious that I'm no businesswoman. I don't know whether it's the hangover but I'm feeling so miserable I toy with the idea of calling Megan to say that I won't be in at all, then decide to try and pull myself together and run a shower.

By the time I actually make it into the shop it's almost 10.30. When she sees me she comes over.

"Are you OK, Kate? You look dreadful. Are you feeling ill?"

"I'm not too good, Megan, to be honest but feeling much better than first thing this morning. Sorry for being late, I had, well, one too many drinks last night."

"Oh Kate, you should be careful. Oh, you poor thing, you really do look terrible. I hope you at least had fun!"

I tell her about the bar, about the conversation with Pete and suddenly out of nowhere I burst into tears.

"What on earth's the matter Kate? Look – you go into the back office, I'll close the shop and we'll have a pot of tea and a chat."

The inexhaustible supply of chocolate chip cookies is back on the table and Megan has just boiled the kettle. I realize that I haven't been completely open with Megan about how I feel. It's not like I've misled her, but for the first time I tell her everything – how I don't think I can face going back to London and how much I'm missing my friends in Panama. I tell her about Nat's idea and Jimmy's uncle's restaurant, about my conversation with Pete and how yesterday afternoon I'd started, for a second, to actually believe that going back to Panama and opening a shop was possible. Then, how I had woken up this morning, not just with a cracking hangover but with the realization that I'll never have the personality, ability and expertise to open a bookshop, not in Panama, not in England, not anywhere.

The tea is brewed and she takes the pot and pours us each a mug while I help myself to the box of tissues she's put on the table and dry my eyes.

"Kate, dear Kate, you really are having a difficult time, aren't you? You're tying yourself up in knots! How long do you think this has all been swimming around up there?" she says, munching on a cookie and pointing a bony finger at my head.

"Well, since Nat mentioned it and then Jimmy showed me his uncle's restaurant…"

"Kate, I think this has all been up there for so much longer," she says, putting the half-eaten cookie down and taking a sip of tea, her half-moon glasses right on the end of her thin, fine nose. They steam up for a second and clear just as quickly as she put the tea down.

"It sounds like you've been unhappy in your job for years, but even then, you've carried this dream around with you, like you never really gave the bookshop idea much credence, like, it was the most impossible thing in the world." She smiles kindly. "You only ever wanted a little second-hand bookshop somewhere Kate, not to go to the moon."

Before I can react, she continues. "Now I don't know London, maybe it did seem an impossible dream back there, and believe me, I know how hard starting up a business can be in a big city like New York, it's expensive and that's just for starters. After all, I was lucky to inherit a good pot of money. Let's not forget that. But now it sounds like you're confronted, for the first time, with the very real possibility that you could make this dream a reality in Panama, and believe me, that's the scariest prospect of all." I know Megan is right. I want to do this so much, but I just don't know if I have it in me.

"Something's stopping you Kate. After all, you know London will always be there. You said yourself that it's easy to find another job in London. But nothing's a prison sentence. What are you afraid of? My guess is that you're afraid of failing – of the whole thing coming crashing down. But honestly, so what if it does? Oh, I'm not being flippant, it'd be disappointing and a hell of a lot of hassle, but really Kate, what have you got to lose when you look at what you've got to gain…?"

"Megan, but if it didn't work out I don't know what I'd do! It's such a big risk!"

"Why wouldn't it work out and why is it such a big risk?" she asks, more sternly now and pushing the plate of biscuits in my direction. I take one, and already I'm feeling a lot better.

"Well, maybe nobody would want to buy English books in Panama, maybe there isn't a big enough market there and I wouldn't make enough money to live off, maybe…"

"But Kate, surely these are all things you can calculate, estimate beforehand, you know, get a feel for the market and do a best- and worst-case scenario?"

"Well, I guess I could have a stab… I used to do that for fundraising, projecting income verses costs…"

"There you go, and you told me that maths isn't your strong point! You've managed it for fundraising for 10 years, this is practically the same. Look Kate, it's now or never and there's no having a stab, you either go for it or you don't. This is a golden opportunity and I'd hate you to miss out and regret it.

"Just the other day I was reading an article in *The Economist*. Panama is really on the upswing. Loads of Americans are retiring down there these days and the Panamanians are investing in the country. They've widened the canal which means more investment and more development in the years to come too. It sounds like Panama is growing, you'd be in the perfect position to take advantage of it and provide something for all these ex-pats moving down there. You told me yourself that there isn't one decent bookshop in the whole city!

"I tell you what, come around to mine tonight. I'll cook us a simple dinner and we'll sit down with a calculator and work it all out – best- and worst-case scenarios, as best we can, with contingency budgets, the lot – all based on you buying Jimmy's uncle's place. I don't know yet if the figures will look good or bad, but at least you'd be informed, and then maybe you can decide, OK?"

"Very OK," I say with a smile as I take another cookie.

15

"Beware; for I am fearless, and therefore powerful."

Frankenstein, Mary Shelley

"Left, right a little, left, perfect!"

"You sure?" I say, looking up.

"Absolutely, we don't want it too near the window. But it can't block the pavement."

Megan has bought a wooden stand for outside the shop where she can display books on a sunny day. It's a sweet addition and in two weeks, the transformation in the shop is almost complete. Megan is so delighted with the way the shop is looking she's decided to re-launch with a new name. Before the shop was called The Lower East Side Bookshop; now it's called The Zola Bookshop, named after her favorite author.

The window is completely clear of books and light is streaming in. Today is particularly sunny, even down this narrow, dim side street. Yesterday, we had the windows cleaned for the first time and the glass is now sparkling like it's just come out of a dish washer and with all the boxes cleared out, the shop is looking much bigger than the day I first came across it. Not only that – there's now a semblance of order on the shelves. It might not be perfect and we're still working on it, but it's a huge improvement.

Megan has decided to have an official "re-opening" with as many people as she can muster: friends, relatives, ex-students and contacts from the university and publishing world. An old friend of Megan's, Margot Lockwood, who has just had her third book published, has agreed to do a reading and book signing, too. It's all pretty impressive and I've discovered that years of lecturing at Columbia means Megan is pretty well connected. Before we know it, she's expecting over 100 people to attend. And then there's Pete. He's coming too. It'll be the first time I've seen him since that night in the bar and it'll be nice to see him and tell him my news.

After I'd had the meltdown in the shop over tea and cookies, I went to Megan's for dinner that night. A few blocks from the shop, Megan lives on the top floor of an old redbrick terrace. They call them "brownstones" in New York. Quite an ordinary place from the outside, once up a steep flight of stairs and through the front door I took in what was a relatively large apartment. An entrance hall with rooms branching off in various directions, wooden floors throughout and furnished with old antique furniture which Megan explained she and her husband picked up on various trips, mainly to Europe, when they were younger. The overwhelming feel is one of quiet, dimly lit tranquility.

Even the floor barely creaked thanks to the many faded Persian rugs scattered almost randomly around. My eyes took a while to adjust, with only three or four desk lamps dotted around here and there to break up the dark. A large grandfather clock was ticking with reassuring reliability in the hall – a notable contrast to sirens and sound of traffic encroaching from the city outside.

Megan led me through to a beautifully cozy and much brighter kitchen. The simple, wooden farmhouse style table was set with two places, a bottle of wine already open.

"Take a seat, Kate. I hope you don't mind dining here? I thought it was cozier and less formal than in the dining room."

I was beginning to realize that Megan has some money. The whole place reeked of quality. Even the wine. I'm no great expert but I know a bottle of Barolo when I see one.

"Of course, this is wonderful. I hope you haven't gone to too much trouble Megan?" I said going over to look at the pot, slowly bubbling on the stove top. It smelled heavenly.

"No, and don't you worry. I love cooking, when I have company that is. Anyway, I've just done a very simple stew with potatoes and green beans. Is that OK?"

"Perfect." I smiled back, taking the glass of wine she passed me and smelling the aromas of Italy and grapes steeped in sunlight.

Something was rubbing round my leg. It was Megan's cat – a beautiful creamy, fluffy looking Siamese. Megan told me that she's a Birman, and that the breed is originally from Burma.

"There's a lovely legend about these cats," Megan explained. "They say that the eyes are blue because centuries ago, the cats were living in Buddhist temples. They were originally white with yellow eyes, so the legend goes. Then one day the temple was attacked by bandits and the head priest was struck down. When he was on the floor dying, a temple cat put his paws onto his master and the priest's soul passed to the cat, and in that instance the cat's eyes changed color from yellow to blue and his coat became this creamy golden color. But his paws remained white, as a sign of purity." She picked up her cat, which she told me is called Mimi, to show me, and she was right. All her paws were white, like she was wearing little socks. I gave her a stroke and she gazed at me through her big blue eyes just as cats do – somehow knowing and indifferent all at the same time. She put her down and she jumped up onto the chair next to me and curled up.

"This is her favorite room in the winter – it's always nice and warm in here. Kate, help yourself to wine as you like. Don't be shy. Dinner's just about ready." I topped up both glasses and we had a quick toast.

"Here's to the future, whatever it holds," she said smiling. "I always say we should follow our dream, wherever they may take us."

We soon ate the very tasty stew and chatted about our favorite authors, books we had recently read and books recently recommended in the *New York Times*. Before long, dinner was finished, the dishes in the sink and we were in her study at the back of the apartment with the last two glasses of wine from the now drained bottle.

The small study was lined wall to wall, ceiling to ceiling with bookshelves, all stuffed with books. I'd always dreamed of owning my own flat with a room just like this. It was quite simply beautiful. I gazed at some of the photos in frames on the desk – photos of Megan in past years with Murray, a handsome man with a thick head of greying hair, glasses and a strong jaw. Through the glasses, I could see very soft, kind eyes. Eyes that look tired through all the reading and years spent in academia.

"He looked like he was a very nice man," I said with sincerity.

"He was a very special human being," she said, picking up one of his photos. "There isn't an hour in the day I don't miss him. Sometimes, I feel like a piece of me has been amputated. It's like trying to walk with just one leg. I know that probably sounds strange but that's the way it feels." She looked wistful, a little sad but as ever, serene. "Anyway, to the matter at hand!"

She soon cleared a space at the table, pushing aside some papers, bills and various documents and pulled out a calculator from the bottom drawer. Once she had pulled up an extra chair for me, she started scribbling down figures and making calculations; the price of the shop, how much I have saved, my grandfather's inheritance which I had put aside and had been planning to use to buy a place for Marco and me, expenses such as electricity, overheads and such like. She pulled out some recent issues of *The Economist* newspaper to show me the articles she remembered seeing and found a few more via a Google search, all of them raving about how Panama was going through an economic boom.

She even suggested I phone up Stuart to ask about the current situation with property right now, numbers of ex-pats currently living in the city and which foreign companies were planning to move there in the near future.

"He's going to love this," I told her, dialing his number. "He's crazy about property and investing in Panama right now."

Stuart was predictably delighted to help and told me all the latest on prices, economic outlook, and the number of Americans estimated to be retiring to Panama in the next five years. I also passed the phone to Meg, who had a few questions of her own. At the end, he promised to keep our conversation confidential and not to tell the others. I didn't want word getting out that I might be coming back to Panama before I had decided for sure. Then Megan started writing down the numbers and seeing how they all stacked up. A lot of it was estimated guess work, but I was impressed at how thorough she was. After what must have been over an hour, she put her pen down and took a large sip of wine.

"This Barolo is great," she said, holding it up to the light to get a better look. "Lovely color, too. You can't beat a good Italian. Well Kate, you know, it's a tricky one. The hardest thing is knowing exactly what the demand would be for books in English in Panama right now, but from what you've said, the shop is in one of the best locations in town and it seems Stuart agrees. You also said he agrees that the price Jimmy's uncle is selling it for is incredibly good. He reckoned that if you sold the place in six months to a year from now, you would make at least 10 percent more on the price, and that could even be higher. He even joked that if you're not interested, he'd consider buying it purely as an investment."

"Really?" I took a large sip from my wine; the glass was now sadly empty.

"So, Kate, to be honest, it's still hard to say if you would make enough money to live off from the business. There are still too many unknowns and variables, but the good news is that, if it didn't work out and you decided to sell in a year, you could potentially be looking at making at least a $20,000 profit, just on the property alone."

"Oh, my goodness. That's incredible!" I was shocked. "I've never really been into property. Investing in real estate was never my thing, but now there's a bookshop at stake I'm beginning to get interested…"

"So, while you have to remember that making a profit on the property alone isn't a given, based on what I've heard, my advice would be that you should use some of your inheritance to buy the restaurant and turn it into a bookshop and take a chance. You can't lose, really, as you know that if the shop doesn't work, you could likely be making a good chunk of money in the long run on the sale. It certainly shouldn't lose you money from what Stuart says."

"Well, I think I'd better give Jimmy a call tomorrow," I said, suddenly feeling worried. Maybe Jimmy had sold it already? Maybe I had missed my chance. These kinds of opportunities don't come along that often.

"I'm definitely giving Jimmy a call."

A few days later, I had to stop working in Megan's bookshop for a few days so I could sort out all my personal stuff related to moving back to Panama. First, I had to phone up my boss in London and tell him that I wouldn't be coming back after all. He was pretty annoyed. He told me through not-so-gritted teeth that he'd turned down a number of really good people for my post and he heard just recently that they've now found other jobs so he would now have to go through a lengthy interview process.

I felt bad. He's been pretty good to me, but I know that I'm making the right choice and that perhaps for the first time in my life I'm thinking just for myself.

Then I had to phone up the shipping company and get them to ship all my stuff back to Panama, but would you believe it, it hadn't even left Panama. It was all still in storage in the container at the port, waiting for the ship to arrive. What a stroke of luck! Then, I booked my flight back and called my old landlord – but that didn't go quite so well, my flat in Panama had already been let to someone else. Jane stepped in, though, and said that I could stay with her until I find my own place. Good old Jane.

And Jane, well, she was jumping for joy at the news.

"I don't believe it Kate, that's wonderful! I can't believe we're getting you back. Wait till I tell the others. We've missed you so much." I also had to phone my mum and dad and Melodie back in London. They were pretty taken aback by my news but as supportive as ever.

When I phoned up Jimmy, he said that luckily his uncle's place was still up for sale. Although there had been a few interested potential buyers, nothing had been signed. Jimmy was, of course, over the moon.

"I'd buy the place myself Kate, but I just don't have the spare cash right now. I've tied it up on other projects. But I'm happy for you. It'll be a great investment! So, when you coming back? I'm leaving for business to China for a couple of weeks tomorrow."

Finding a place to live will be the main priority when I get back there but Jane has said I can stay as long as I like with her. For a moment, the thought of organizing all this and whatever else awaits is overwhelming. My Spanish still isn't great and no doubt there'll be plenty of Panamanian bureaucracy involved in getting visas and opening a business, but Jimmy promised to help out as soon as he's back from China. I'm so excited about this challenge, so buzzed to be seeing all my friends in Panama…

Megan is making us coffee and the catering company have just arrived for tonight's re-opening of her bookshop and is asking where we are going to set up the table for nibbles and drinks. There's still a lot of work to do here, but I'm walking on air. And before you know it, the opening is in full swing…

"Thank you all for coming tonight," Megan begins. "I so appreciate your support. As you can see, we are happy to be re-launching my wonderful bookshop. I know it's only a second-hand bookshop, not a fancy type of Barnes & Noble affair, but well, I hope you like it as much as me.

"A few highlights to point out: We have an amazing selection of modern American poetry on the left, the Penguin Classics section right behind you is also very interesting and our specialty – modern American fiction – is just to your left.

"But before you all get back to browsing and I hope another glass of wine or two, I'd just like to introduce you to Kate if you haven't met her already. Kate is from England and has helped me so much over the last few weeks. In fact, if it wasn't for Kate, we wouldn't be here now celebrating this re-launch. I'd still be struggling through boxes and I'm sure a few of you remember what it was like in here before Kate arrived on the scene. Those of you who do remember will be able to see how much she has helped with this transformation. She was up even until midnight last night, preparing for tonight, so thank you, Kate. Thank you so much. I couldn't've done it without you."

As everybody claps, I turn the color of my glass of Bordeaux. Megan continues.

"And another piece of news – Kate will be leaving us in four days to start a new life in Panama City where she plans to open up a shop of her very own. So let's toast Kate in her new adventure!"

All eyes are on me and for a moment I'm so embarrassed I don't know where to look. "Good luck Kate!" and everyone raises their glasses.

"So please stay as long as you like, tonight we are open until the last customer leaves. As I said, have another glass of wine and please feel free to ask me any questions – especially if you are looking for something in particular. Oh, and another very big thanks to Margot for her reading tonight. Margot is going to be here for another hour and can sign copies of her book, which she has brought along. That's right, isn't it Margot?"

"Sure, Megan. I'll be here until 9.30," says Margot Lockwood, nodding and smiling around.

The crowd breaks up and immediately, there's lively chatter and conversation. I turn up the volume on a jazz CD we have playing in the background ever so slightly. The atmosphere is so cozy and my cheeks are glowing – either it's the warm atmosphere, the wine or both. There has been a good turnout, with people drifting in and out throughout the night. Megan has sold more books in this one night than in the last month. Pete arrived in the middle of Margot's reading and stayed at the back, listening with a concentrated frown, until he saw me and grinned over the heads of the small crowd.

I'd told Megan about Pete the barman and she insisted we invite him. It seemed a little strange to call him and tell him about the re-launch party; after all, I don't really know him at all but Megan was very persistent.

After Megan's speech I can see he's making his way over from the entrance and when he reaches us at the counter, I introduce him to Megan.

"Well, very nice to meet you, Pete. Kate told me you wrote a book which is set here in New York?"

"Yes, I'm afraid nothing published yet, though," he says looking for a moment shyer than I could have imagined. "Although at least I have an agent now," he adds.

"Well, maybe Kate told you that I used to teach literature at Columbia, so if you want some time, I'd love to have a look at your manuscript. And I know a few publishers too…"

"That would be great!" he says, nodding enthusiastically. "I'd really value your opinion. I just can't get it published, I've been trying all year and I'm beginning to wonder if I've got what it takes. My agent is very supportive and is convinced he can make it happen but your candid opinion would be really appreciated right now."

"Well, you bring it along here and I can sit and read it while I'm in the shop. Next week, can you pop it in?"

"Sure, I'll bring it over. I nearly brought a copy tonight but thought, well, that it was a bit presumptuous."

"Not at all, young man," she says, shaking her head. "And see that guy over there?" she continues, nodding in the direction of a man chatting with a group of women. "He's in publishing, owns his own small independent company. From memory, he's very fond of the crime genre. Shall I introduce you?"

"Sure, that would be great!" says Pete enthusiastically. She takes him over and before long, they're engaged in a friendly, lively conversation.

Some time later, Pete comes back with a smile on his face, clutching a business card.

"He wants me to send him my manuscript!"

"Wonderful, now where are you two going tonight for dinner? I assume you'll be off having dinner somewhere nice?" says Megan, with a wicked glint in her eye.

Pete hadn't actually asked me out to dinner and for a moment I am mortified, but he steps in glancing at me.

"Well, Kate, I was wondering if I could take you to dinner later at a great place I know around the corner, Pier Luigi? Do you like Italian food?"

"Love it," I say, blushing and feeling suddenly a little awkward – like I've somehow been set up. How did that happen – Pete taking me to dinner? Trust Megan and her big mouth. I quickly add: "But we're going to hang around a while here first, right Pete?"

"Sure," he nods, looking around. "Great place, by the way, I'd love some time to take a proper look."

"Oh yes Kate, Pier Luigi is a great place for pasta," adds in Megan. "You'll love it. But really Kate, you've already done so much. Please feel free to go when you like. I'll finish off here tonight."

It isn't that I'm not happy to be having dinner with Pete, as I said, he's cute and a really interesting guy. In fact, this impromptu dinner is a great unexpected turn-up for the books, but I am also lapping up the atmosphere in the shop tonight. Megan and I have worked so hard to get to this point and I want to savor every moment. There are still around 30 people here and the place is buzzing with literary conversation – a small group is talking to Margot, others are chatting and drinking wine, there are also people browsing the shelves and three waiting to pay for some books. Megan is now back at the till, beaming and trying to serve each customer as quickly as possible, but with many friends and contacts in the group, the queue isn't going down quickly – they all want to congratulate her on the re-launch.

I feel so lucky to have met Megan, with her open approach to life. She took me on here in this shop and it has had a major impact on my life. I don't think I would have ever made the decision to go back to Panama – let alone open up my own shop – without spending the last three weeks in here.

"Shall we go?" Pete asks. It's getting late and he's already had some long chats to a number of people, lecturers, students, teachers and one other writer and he is now glancing over at me.

"Sure, let's make a move," I smile back, suddenly feeling shy.

We leave the chattering, cozy atmosphere of the shop and head out into the cold night air. The restaurant is a few blocks south but I'm immediately put at my ease as we walk over there. Pete and I continue talking, laughing, somehow already really getting on – seems we have so much to talk about, so much in common, he's easy company.

Pier Luigi has a very chilled atmosphere. We take the only remaining table and before long we've ordered some wine and our starters. Over dinner I decide I was right about Pete. He's a really nice guy. We chat about life in New York and London. What he does and doesn't miss about Phoenix and where he grew up in Ohio and how he got a passion for literature and eventually started writing his first book. He seems genuinely interested in me. He asks me so many questions about this and that, that by the end of the evening I feel like I've been interviewed on a TV chat show, but it's so refreshing that I lose track of time completely and the restaurant is closing by the time the tired waiters say goodbye.

We decide to get a night cap in a local bar and descend into a comfy leather sofa. It's so soft and warm and somehow, I find we're leaning into each other more and more.

"So, Kate, you're leaving in four days to start a new life in Panama? Just my luck!" he says smiling.

"Yes, life's funny isn't it? By now I was supposed to be back in London, in my old job with New York and Panama a distant memory and of course I wouldn't have met you and well, we wouldn't be sitting here now…"

"I can't believe you're such a quick mover!" he says putting down his drink and fixing me with a strong gaze. "When I met you the other night you were just talking about missing Panama, and that you were worried you were making a mistake going back to London and here we are 10 days later and it's all booked. You're going back!"

He was right. I'd surprised even myself. It had taken me a long while to realize what I wanted, but once I had, my mind was made up and I wasn't wasting any more time.

"Can I see you again, before you leave?" he asks.

"Look, I really like you a lot Pete, I like you very much but well, you know that this is very bad timing for me. I'm only here for four more nights – you know, I'm leaving for Panama next Tuesday…"

"Yes, I know. It's crazy. Bad timing. But well, I'd really like to see you again. Can't we?"

"I've got so much to do…" I resist.

"Like what?" he asks directly.

"Pack and well, pack…"

"Come on, surely that's not going to take you too long!" he laughs out loud.

"And tomorrow night I'm taking Patricia and Mike out for dinner to say thanks for having me and then on Sunday I'm having a farewell dinner with Megan."

"I have to work anyway. It's the worst thing about being a barman, no time off in the evenings. But I can meet you for drinks after. I know loads of nice places we could go – you know, we are in the city that never sleeps," he says, fixing my gaze. "Come on, we could check out some new bars – research for my next book," he grins.

"Well, I guess we *could* meet up again… I mean…"

"Great – I knew you'd see sense!" He laughs before I can change my mind. He gives my hand a squeeze. I realize just then that the squeeze is lasting longer than, well, a squeeze…

"Oh no!" I think. And my heart does an ever so small back flip.

16

"It's never too late to be wise."

Robinson Crusoe, Daniel Defoe

The rain is driving against the taxi window, its wiper working hard to clear a path through the deluge as it bounces off the glass and back up into the torrent. Silver-white. Heavy drops. It's a grey day and getting darker although that's hard to imagine as my eyes focus on the heavy charcoal tarmac stretching off on the freeway ahead. I'm leaving New York. I turn to take a look at the sweeping view out of the rear window. I could cusp the buildings, already model sized, in my hand. It's comforting somehow. That the city is receding into an imaginary palm size model in my hand.

As the taxi pulls up at the airport, I turn to look at Pete. It's just a second really as without a word he jumps out of the cab to start organizing my modest collection of suitcases.

His hand had been warm and firm in my grip in the taxi. Through the Lincoln Tunnel. Over the flyovers and along the freeway.

Pete the barman and writer. Pete the kind, sweet, generous, funny guy who made me an Electric Lemonade cocktail and unknowingly helped me to write the next chapter of my life. And it seems the first page of his own next chapter has been turned, too.

The morning after the bookstore re-opening, he had a call from his agent. Seems with recent re-writes, a publisher is interested in Frankie Nero now. Seems detective novels are getting more popular again. Seems they think that with just a little more work, Frankie Nero could be a goer. He showed me his manuscript the very next day, tentatively, taking a deep breath of insecurity as I read just the first few pages. I told him to prepare himself – he's going to be the next big thing in crime writing.

"You know I'm going to really miss you," he says. "It's been wonderful – the last week, meeting you, spending time together. Hell, I can't believe it – that you're leaving today…" We are standing in front of the check-in desk and my luggage has just jolted off bouncing merrily down the conveyer belt destined for Panama. Pete's words trail off like the luggage not yet knowing their final destination.

"I know, it's come around really quickly. The last few days have just flown by," I admit.

Could it be that Pete is moved, sad that I'm leaving? I have to keep it light. I've too much on my plate to get emotionally involved right now.

"And I was just getting used to being around myself!" I continue, smiling up at him and he hesitates, he opens his mouth for a second, but thinks again. He smiles back and I respect him the more.

It's hard to explain what has exactly happened between Pete and me. In fact, nothing's really happened. Not even a kiss. Well I suppose a bit of semi-romance – but certainly nothing in the bedroom department. I had the sense he wanted to kiss me a couple of times. But I've been giving off conflicting messages and he also told me the other night that he's just broken up with a long-term girlfriend. So, I've been keeping him at arm's length and I don't think he's ready for anything to develop with me either. Timing.

It's often about timing. Having said that there's a strong feeling, a strong something between us that's hard to define. It's more than friendship. He sighs, looks away as if taking a few moments to collect his thoughts.

"Look, you've got a lot on your plate right now with this move back to Panama and I don't want to make it worse… I just really want you to know well… that I'm glad we met and I hope that we'll stay in touch. I'd love to come and visit you like we discussed – as soon as you're settled and I've saved up the cash… anyway, have a great flight – call me when you get settled in. Let me know how you're doing, won't you?"

"Of course," I say as he gives me the biggest, tightest hug.

"And I can't wait to hear how the meeting goes with your agent and the publishing house. My fingers will be crossed for you. Did he give any indication on the re-writes, like how extensive they should be?" I ask.

"He said minor, but well, his idea of minor might not be mine," he grins.

"Goodbye, Pete." And I pull away and walk to the security check. I wave him goodbye and he waves back from the other side.

Maybe it's my imagination but for a moment he looks lonely in the bustle of the departure hall – still and forlorn where it seems the world is hurrying around him, crisscrossing in infinite directions to the many check-in counters and security checks.

The whole world seems to be on the move sometimes. I give him a wave and he waves back before turning on his heels and heading out of the airport and for a moment I'm slightly disappointed when he doesn't glance back.

The arrival hall at Tocumen airport is another matter. As I step out through the sliding doors and into the arrival hall I'm greeted by screams and a louder-than-life cheer – Jane, Nat, Beth, May, Stuart and Paco rush forward and I feel like I'm going to be wonderfully squashed by this overflow of emotion and excitement.

"Yeay!!!! Welcome back!" screams Jane running over, giving a huge hug. "I can't believe you're here!"

"How was the flight?" asks Nat wrapping me, and Jane by default, in a big squeeze. How many hugs can a girl take in one day? Paco has gone mad and is jumping up and down. I bend down and give him a cuddle on the tummy as he rolls over on the floor excitedly, tail wagging. It's nice to be home. I'm home!

I'm soon in Beth's car with my luggage in the boot, zipping along the dark strip of a motorway in her snazzy soft top MG, back to the city, the lights of the modern skyscrapers glimmering in the distance and fast approaching. They look positive and bright in contrast to the dark, heavy grey towers in New York.

I breathe in the night air. It smells strongly of freshly dampened, tropical earth – it's probably just rained and I feel a swell of excitement. No more bracing, frosty winds and freezing air. And if it rains, who cares? The rain is like liquid sunshine here. And the heat. I can feel and smell the heat. Yes, even the heat has its very own perfume in Panama it seems.

It's quite late but I'm not at all tired. I'm feeling alive and buzzing with energy. I'm like an electric wire that's just been plugged in and has a current pulsing through its veins.

"Guys, how about a drink in *Plaza Bolivar*. Bar Blanca?" I ask turning around to look at Jane and May in the back seat.

"Of course," says Jane. "We wouldn't expect anything less. Let me text Nat and Stuart. I think they're behind in Stuart's car. I'll tell them to meet us directly in the bar."

We quickly pass by Jane's place, drop off my luggage and head to Bar Blanca for celebration drinks.

"*Hola Chica*!" says Ricky, coming over and giving me a hug and kiss on each cheek.

"Good to see you, it's not the same here without the mad English book woman. What can I get you?"

"That's easy. An Electric Lemonade for me!" I say pulling over a chair and sitting down with a huge smile on my face.

"So here you are!" says Jane as we sit down, "Never thought we were going to get you back. But hey, it's great. I still can't believe it!"

"Thanks so much for putting me up Jane, I really appreciate it," I say. "I'm going to start looking for something to rent immediately. Stuart, you still think it's a good move, buying in Panama I mean? Nothing's changed in a week that I should know about?" I'm joking but Stuart takes these things very seriously.

"Sure is," he says with a nod. "Prices are still going up so you'd be wise to buy as soon as possible. I've been telling everyone for months…"

"Here we go again!" says Jane, giving Stuart an affectionate shove.

"And then I need to get everything sorted out – with Jimmy's uncle's place. He's in China right now but he left me the telephone number of his uncle and a lawyer he recommended and…"

"Jimmy's uncle's place?" Beth interrupts. "Sorry, Kate, what are you talking about?"

"Oh, didn't I mention?"

I realize now that I didn't really go into detail on the phone when I called Jane. Jimmy left for China and probably hasn't had a moment to mention it to anyone either.

"I've decided to take up Nat's idea and try to open up a bookshop. It might take me a while but, in the meantime, I figure that I can always fall back on teaching English. A lot of it was to do with the fact that Jimmy's uncle is selling his restaurant. It's just around the corner. I can show you later or tomorrow. Anyway, he's agreed to sell it to me at a really good price. Then I'll have to fit it out, like a bookshop and that will take a bit of time and a bit of investment…"

Everyone is looking at me very uneasily. The atmosphere has suddenly changed. I can sense it. Nobody says a word. Beth is looking uncomfortably at Jane.

"What's going on?" asks Stuart, fixing Jane with a stare, glancing back at Beth with a question mark on his face and then back to Jane. There's another long pause. I take a sip of my Electric Lemonade.

"What's up?"

"Kate, do you remember Linda?" Jane says slowly.

"Linda, who's Linda?" I ask taking another sip and enjoying the taste like never before.

"Don't you remember Linda from when we went to the San Blas islands?"

"Oh, that awful American woman from Colorado? What's her husband called, Tim? No, it's Tom, yes, Tom. He was quite nice. Anyway, what about her?"

"Kate, Linda and Tom have decided to come here much sooner. They arrived here a week ago. I met with her just two nights ago. She's planning to open a bookshop in *Casco Viejo.*"

I know I've been naïve. I know I've been stupid. How could I have forgotten about Linda and her plans to move to *Casco Viejo* and open up a bookshop!? The fact that she's come early and is already putting her plans into action is the worst-case scenario, of course, but even then, if she were coming in six months, as she originally planned, it would still be pretty bad. She wouldn't have been too happy to arrive here to see that I'd pipped her to the post.

Casco Viejo is so tiny. How on earth will two bookshops survive here? It'll be hard enough for one. In any case the worst scenario is upon me. I'm about to start my new business; buy Jimmy's uncle's restaurant, and Linda is already here searching for her own commercial space to do exactly the same. What on earth am I going to do?

The evening ended on this very sour note although I had tried to skim over it. I certainly came back down to earth with a sharp and more-than-uncomfortable bump. Jane told me that Tom and Linda have bought a flat in *Casco* and are now on the hunt for a commercial space – either to rent or buy. It won't take them long, Stuart tells me. There are loads of commercial spaces to rent right now and monthly rentals are super low.

Everyone had their own piece of advice:

Jane said I should meet with Linda and have a frank chat, tell her my plans then go our separate ways, do our own thing.

Beth thought I should meditate, meet with Linda, give her a hug (you know, the kind you normally give to trees) and suggest we go into business together.

Stuart's opinion was that two bookshops in such a small area would be a commercial a disaster but didn't have much to say after that.

Nat thinks two bookshops would be better and draw in more business in the longer term.

Paco didn't have anything to say on the topic but his tail wagged a little less enthusiastically. I took that as a less than positive sign.

There was a lot of talk and debate but the main thing is that they are all supportive of me and my plans and at the end of the evening on my way back to Jane's flat, I was once again reminding myself how lucky I am to have such good friends.

It's the morning after, Jane is out meeting a potential client for some web design thing, and I make myself a boiled egg and double expresso coffee. I sit on her small patio. Jane has green fingers and every bit of available space is a mass of bright tropical plants in large terracotta tubs. She's left Linda's business card on the side – so I can call her if I want. I finger it as I drink my cappuccino turning it over and over in my hand, my mind turning with it as I try to collect my thoughts. My next move is an important one. Whatever happens, I need Linda as my friend, not as a business rival or worse my enemy. The world is small and *Casco Viejo* is like a very small pond in a smaller than average garden. I know that I have to call her, to arrange to meet up but I keep putting it off. I'm terrified. Eventually, it's almost 11am and I call her.

It's 12.30pm the next day and I'm sitting in the very sumptuous setting of the restaurant at the Vista Del Mar Hotel. Positioned right by the main marina in the bay, in the heart of Panama City, and with a view down on to the large kidney shaped swimming pool a couple of levels below it's a perfect setting for brunch and on pleasantly neutral territory outside *Casco*. Linda is late. I'm already on my first glass of something fizzy that tastes like champagne but isn't.

Eventually I see Linda arrive. She makes her way over to my table and I feel mildly sick. I ask the waiter for a top up and feel like I'll need a few more before the lunch is over.

"Hi there Linda," I get up and shake her hand as warmly as I can muster of myself. She goes further and reaches over to give me a kiss on the cheeks and a somewhat theatrical embrace.

"Hello my dear, I never thought I'd see you again! Last I heard was that you were on a plane back to London."

She sits down and I feel so intimidated by her brash, heavy make-up, weighty gold jewelry and brassy hair. She motions to the waiter to bring her some champagne too and for a second, I get the impression she's nervous. I imagine her mind has been racing about what I'm doing back here. Why I want to meet.

"So, Kate," she says taking a long sip of champagne.

"As I was saying, I heard from Jane that you'd gone back to London. Before we moved here, we stayed in touch by email. Then the other day she told me you were coming back. I asked her why but she just said that you were missing Panama. So, you can imagine, it's lovely to see you! Seems like so long ago now that we were all on the San Blas islands together. And I'd love to hear what you have planned, and also why you want to meet with me?"

She's perfectly civil, calm and mild mannered, but underneath I wonder if she's guessed – if she knows that I'm planning to open a bookshop?

"Well Linda, thanks first for meeting with me. It's nice now that I'm back to know that as we're going to be living in Panama maybe we can do this more often – brunch I mean." I'm babbling and I know it. I have no intention of socializing with Linda unless I have to, so I decide to take a deep breath and try without success to get to the point. "… and how have you been? How was the move?"

She launches into what seems like an hour-long monologue about leaving the US, packing up the family home, leaving parties, and Tom's golf club do. All the tears of her family and friends and I start to zone out. If I wasn't so nervous I'd be yawning. Eventually she pauses for breath and I take the opportunity to suggest we grab some food from the extensive buffet.

Laid out on long tables is an amazing selection of food – anything you could imagine wanting to eat for brunch. Fresh seafood including prawns, salmon, lobster, crab, roast leg of pork and beef with all the trimmings, numerous salads, breakfast things and a table of deserts to die for.

Back at our table, with glasses topped up by the ever-attentive waiting staff, I attack a small plate of super huge prawns during which, seeing Linda has her mouth full, I decide to launch in while I have the chance.

"Actually Linda, I hope you don't mind me changing the subject but today I didn't just want to catch up with you socially, nice enough as this is, but I also wanted to meet with you over business."

"Business?" she says her mouth and jaw line stiffening as she chews.

"Well, maybe you remember that we talked weeks ago about how we both wanted to open a bookshop in *Casco Viejo*?"

"Well, no Kate. It wasn't exactly like that. I remember very well. You told me you'd thought about it and decided against and that you were going back to London. I on the other hand I told you that I was going to come to Panama and do it. And, well, here I am!"

She smiles, takes a sip of champagne, but it's a stressed smile. She takes another sip and I can see a sticky, glossy, fuchsia pink lipstick mark on the glass.

"Well that might be true Linda, but the reason I wanted to meet with you today is to tell you that I'm back in Panama because I've changed my mind. You see, on my way back to London, I re-thought the whole thing and decided to come back, and that's why I wanted to meet with you today…"

"You've changed your mind?" She suddenly looks stern, putting down her glass and fixing me across the table.

"Kate if you don't mind I think you owe me an explanation. You know that I am planning to open a bookshop in Casco and you think that you can just turn up here and tell me that you are going to do the same thing? I've been planning this for months… also on the basis that there isn't a bookshop here…"

"Look, Linda, to be honest I completely forgot about you and your plans. I was in New York and well a few things happened which made me realize that the bookshop was what I wanted to do, all I ever wanted to do, and I got excited, booked my ticket back and it wasn't until the other night, after I got back that Jane reminded me about you and your plans and that in fact you'd already arrived…"

"That's rubbish!" she snaps. She's getting angry now; I can see beads of sweat trying to break out on her top lip, hard for them, given the amount of foundation she's wearing.

"You knew exactly what you were doing and I don't believe you'd forgotten about me for a second." I can see a purple vein sticking out on the side of her forehead and even in this air-conditioned environment I can see small beads of sweat on her neck now too.

"Look Linda, I don't want to argue with you. We both want to open a bookshop in *Casco Viejo* and we are both here to stay. So, let's try working together on this to find a solution rather than…"

"No way Kate! I was here first and I'm going ahead and if you think I'm even giving you the time of day again you are very much mistaken. How dare you come back to Panama and steal my idea! I don't think you even had the idea until you met me!"

"No Linda, please, that just isn't true… ask Jane…" but before I can finish, she picks up her bag, throws her napkin down on the table.

"Linda, listen, please sit down and be reasonable. Let's talk this thing through and surely we can work something out." I sound like

I'm pleading now but she's not listening, fiddling with the clasp on her bag. It's a Gucci.

"Kate, goodbye. Please don't contact me again." And before I can answer, she storms out of the restaurant without so much as a glance back in my direction.

"More champagne, signora?" says the waiter who is passing the table.

"Yes please," I say trying to smile and it occurs to me that to cap it all I'll have to cover her bill.

17

"I've never known any trouble that an hour's reading didn't assuage."

Charles De Secondat

"Come on Kate, you should be enjoying this moment, not feeling stressed!" I tell myself irritably, wishing that Stuart were here and wondering where he is. He's never normally late.

"Sign here and here." The notary points to two places on the official document with his pen and passes it to me. I take it and sign. The notary's office is small and cramped, the air thick and oppressive. There are no windows – just a bright florescent light in the middle of the ceiling with some dead flies attached to it with others circling in a languid manner, not even making a buzz to break the sound of the ceiling fan overhead.

I'm sweating under my clothes. I feel a bead of perspiration run down my spine and imagine a cool shower washing away this and the grime of the city. But today I can't entirely blame the city and climate for my discomfort. The anxiety of signing these deeds is causing my body to react and underscores the level of my commitment, for today I'm signing deeds for Jimmy's uncle's place which right now, with the movement of my pen scratching across official paper is becoming "my place". I feel like I'm signing my life away and feel weighed down and elated by it all at the same time.

I hand the pen back and give the notary an unconvincing smile. He disregards my gaze and stony-faced waves his assistant over.

"Take copies for Signora Lewis." The assistant takes the deeds and disappears through a side door.

"Please wait in the reception. Your copies will take just a few minutes. Thank you, Signora Lewis, my invoice will be sent to you by email." And with that he shakes my hand firmly, ushers me out of his office, back to the reception and is soon waving another client through.

While I wait for my copies, I begin feeling calmer. Stuart was right. My money has gone so much further here than back in London and I've still got a nice sum in the bank for a rainy day. I've also found a great flat to rent – it's cute with a small kitchen and living room, mezzanine bedroom and small roof terrace. Stuart tried to persuade me to buy somewhere to live too, but one property is enough for me right now. The flat is nice though. It's just been renovated and it now means I can get my stuff out of storage and move right in.

Jimmy's uncle's place is a different matter and needs work to turn it into my dream bookshop. I've already spoken to a friend of Beth's who is an interior architect and for a small fee, he's going to help me renovate and refurbish the place. I'm keen to get started, but the renovation is just the beginning, I need permits, visas, and most of all stock. Some of my own huge collection will be sacrificed for the second-hand books section, but I've decided to also stock new books, so that I will be able to supply new titles, best sellers and the books many people search for on a holiday or simply at home with the need for something good to read.

I can see a few headaches ahead. Signing these deeds is just the beginning but I'm ready to crack on and make a go of it.

Since brunch a month ago, a lot has been happening in my life and I haven't had much time to worry about Linda, but I'd be lying if I didn't admit to the fact that it's always on the back of my mind.

Casco Viejo is such a small place and I never know when I'm going to bump into her. I keep expecting to walk down a street and spot her coming in my direction, or worse even – to turn a corner and walk right into her. But I'll just have to cross that bridge when I come to it. Jane meets up with her from time to time and tells me that she's still looking for the right space to rent and hasn't found it yet, so I'm ahead of her in the game and although I shouldn't I just can't help getting a strange sense of satisfaction out of that. My cell phone is buzzing and I see it's Stuart.

"Hi Kate, I'm so sorry. Are you still there? I'm stuck in traffic on Calle 50. I might be here for some time – I don't know what's going on, the road is completely jammed…"

"Hey Stuart, look – don't worry, it's all done and I'm going to leave in a few minutes. I was just about to call you."

"Oh god, I'm so sorry Kate! It's my fault. If I'd known that the traffic was going to be so bad I would've left an hour ago. There must've been an accident. It's never normally so bad, even in the rain." He sounds really frazzled and I suddenly feel rather guilty at asking him to come along. I managed on my own and really didn't need the moral support after all.

"Really Stuart, it's no problem. I'm sorry you're stuck in this jam."

"Everything OK though?" he asks.

"Everything's fine. I just signed and I now own a place in *Casco Viejo*!" I'm sure he can see me smiling down the phone.

"Fantastic Kate! We have to celebrate big time!"

"But you're coming for dinner tonight at Jane's, right?" I ask.

"Of course, wouldn't miss it for the world, and I'm bringing two bottles of bubbly," he responds with typical Stuart enthusiasm.

"Ok, see you later, about 8. OK?"

"Great, see you then," he says before hanging up.

I say goodbye to the receptionist, grab a cab outside the notary just in time to dodge a seasonal downpour, and I'm soon speeding along the seafront breathing in the morning air. It's a cocktail of car fumes, rotting sewage, rain and god knows what else. I take a breath and try not to take another and wind up the window. It's really pungent today.

The taxi driver is crazy but then each taxi ride is a trip which transports your heart into your mouth and back down again, with their crazy driving and beat up cars. I'm sometimes glad when the traffic is bad – at least the speeds are reduced as the traffic becomes a crawl. That way I'm more likely to survive the trip.

As my taxi jostles for position at the traffic lights I catch sight of one of the buses that used to be common here.

These *Diavolo Roja* or Red Devils as they are called by the locals, were the transport here a few years back, so they say, replaced now by modern air-conditioned varieties, but a few are still around – and I like them. They are garishly customized by their owners in psychedelic spray-can art and feature anything from the faces of musicians, film stars and cartoon characters. As the bus in front pulls away and the black noxious exhaust fumes clear, I see a scene of the Swiss Alps and Snoop Dog's portrait on the emergency exit of this one.

It's almost lunchtime and I jump from the cab just before *Casco Viejo* to get some fresh seafood from the local market. Tonight, I'm having everyone round to dinner at Jane's place to celebrate the closing of the deal of my shop and signing a one-year lease on an apartment – and I want to give people a feast. A few dollars are all I need to put on this seafood banquet and I'm not sparing any cash today. I want the best.

A huge black woman, bulging from her tight shorts and skimpy t-shirt and with large pink curlers in her hair, beckons me over to where she's sitting on the entrance steps, set back a little from the bustling, noisy crowds. She tries to tempt me with a fresh pineapple juice – a dollar a cup, but the smell of fish from inside the market is so overwhelming I couldn't take a sip of anything right now.

The market is a hive of activity. I wander around the stalls trying to find fresh lobster and eventually, ignoring the calls of stall holders, I see some fresh langoustines – small local lobster with no claws, more like enormous prawns. I negotiate a price for eight and while the stall owner is pushing the slowly protesting creatures into a large blue carrier bag, feeling bad and not wanting to look, I wander around to see what else is on offer. It's an overwhelming display of fish and the prices are so good I'm tempted to get more for the entire week but Jane's fridge is already full so I take just what I need for tonight – along with the langoustines, sea bass to make a ceviche (lemon marinated fish) – and head back to *Casco* through the vibrant, noisy, colorfully port. Who knows what deals take place here. Many foreigners don't walk here and I suppose it is a little bit "edgy" but then, Panama is safer than most countries in the region and I'm somehow confident these days.

Back at Jane's I soon start busying myself in the kitchen and I pull out my one and only Panamanian cookery book. It's going to be fun hosting my first dinner party and I'm already planning many more when I finally get the keys to my new flat. I'm engrossed in a receipt for Sancocho – a typical Panamanian soup – which sounds perfect to start, followed by the ceviche and langoustines, when the intercom buzzes.

"Hi, is that Kate?" the voice on the intercom sounds strained, nervous even, but familiar.

"Yes, it's Kate, who is this?"

"It's Linda, I'd errr, well, I wonder… do you have a moment? I'd like to talk…"

We take a seat at Bar Blanca in *Plaza Bolivar* and order drinks. I order a coffee and Linda, a rum cocktail. From the look on her face she needs something to calm her nerves.

"So, Kate, it seems that we didn't really get off to a good start, you I, I mean…" This time I'm determined to not let her push me around and I'm wondering more and more what she's doing here, why she wants to speak to me now.

"Well, I guess you could put it like that." I interrupt. I look

149

at Linda across the table. Our table is in the shade of a big tree which is blowing in a light but warm breeze. As the dappled shadow crosses her face and patches of sunlight seep through, Linda suddenly looks older than her years. For a moment I see a softness to her face that I've never seen before. She runs her fingers through her hair and the grey roots show themselves. I suddenly feel my heart soften to a woman who for the first time appears almost vulnerable, even frail.

"Look Kate, I really want to apologize – you know, how I behaved before, the other month. I was bang out of line. You have every right, just like me, to open a bookshop in *Casco*. And well, I saw Jane the other day and she told me that you'd been thinking about it long before you even met me, that it was your dream and it was while you were away in New York that you suddenly decided that you actually have the courage to do it, and well, it was nothing to do with me.

"I think I just felt, well, it's hard to explain, like you had stolen my idea and, I guess to be honest Kate, I felt threatened and that you were in 'my space'. I panicked. I was overwhelmed with this fear that if you opened a bookshop, well, that it would be a big success and mine would… well, fail and… I know it's no excuse for the way I spoke to you, walking out on you like that…"

"Linda, apology accepted." I smile across at her. For a moment I feel like I understand exactly how she felt. I would've probably felt just the same. I soften some more.

"Look Linda, so we didn't get off to a good start, but part of that is my fault. To be really honest I guess when I first met you I felt threatened by you too – this whole bookshop thing, I don't know, I just felt upset that you were going to do it and not me, but I swear, at that point I really had decided to go back to London and when I decided to come back here from New York, I don't know why, but I completely forgot about you and your plans, which is crazy I know but I got so carried away with the idea… anyway, I never ever wanted to step on your toes, cause trouble and ruin your plans. You have every right to open a bookshop here too. In fact, you decided to do it before me. So look, I quite understand."

We are both reflective for a second or two then she's smiling and she holds up her glass.

"I would like to propose a toast to us, to letting bygones be bygones, to starting again and... well, I have two motives for coming to see you today. First, I really wanted to apologize and try to make a fresh start with you.

"But also, well, I have a proposition for you, a business proposition. Kate, I've been thinking, maybe this is a crazy idea, but what do you think about pooling our resources, about doing this bookshop together?"

For a moment I am stunned. So, this is why she'd come seeking me out, to put this proposition to me. I suddenly feel suspicious. What isn't she telling me? Couldn't she find a suitable space to buy or rent? Does she have other complications like finance problems? But before I can open my mouth she carries on.

"Kate, I know exactly what you're thinking, like there's something behind this, my finances aren't up to it, I can't find a shop, but it's not that. In fact, today I almost signed on the rental contract of a great space right over there." She points across the square where an empty commercial space is sitting, tantalizing. I have to admit, it is a top location and it beats mine hands down. Right on the main square, great foot fall. All the tourists pass here.

"And my finances are in top shape, I just sold a ton of highly sought-after art in Colorado. In fact, I can afford to buy that space or one like it if I wanted. No, it's nothing like that, but simply that, well, I got to thinking about my retirement. This bookshop was supposed to be fun, a nice project to give me something to keep me occupied, meet people, but well, I've been thinking a lot about it recently Kate. I've talked to Tom. I don't want all the stress involved with it. I'd much rather do it with a partner, share the burden if you know what I mean. Given that you are here too with the same idea, why not pool our resources, ease the strain? I'm sure it'll be more fun too, to have someone to do this with rather than doing it all alone."

"Umm, well Linda, I see your point. It's just a little bit, well, unexpected for me. I have to think about it. You know that I've just bought a place and invested in that and well, I don't know. I just have to think about if it's what I want, you know, to share this project. I need to make a living out of it too – it's not some retirement game for me."

"Oh, I see. But well, you will give it some consideration?" she asks, looking humble all of a sudden. I think for a second. I'm tempted to say no right there and then. But something stops me.

"OK, look, I guess I can think about it. I'll give it some thought over the next few days and well, I'll let you know." I say finishing my drink and adding, "As you can imagine, I need some time to think it through properly. After we last met, I wasn't really expecting this." Not that I really need to explain myself...

"Well, I'll give you a buzz in a couple of days, if that's OK?" she asks.

"Sure, that's fine, Linda." I stand up to signal the end of our meeting and hold out my hand. She smiles and we shake.

"Call me at the weekend. OK?" I say. "But look, sorry I have to dash now, I've got a dinner tonight at a ton of things to do."

"Speak to you soon Kate," she says, grabs her bag and heads off down the street.

I take the long route back to Jane's along the former ramparts of the old city in order to think. I sit on an old iron cannon and take in the view. The sun is setting across the bay and the sky is clear, a few pink wisps of cloud slowly settling in giving additional color to the horizon. Looking down, the tide is out and the sunset is reflected up in the many rock pools and wet sand. Turning it over in my mind I can see Linda's point. At retiring age she probably wants an easy life and has just realized how much work opening a bookshop in Panama would be. I think back to Megan in New York and her struggle and imagine Linda in the same position. She must be about the same age, camouflaged by peroxide and make-up, but give or take a few years, more or less the same. I'm divided, torn, but I can't take Linda up on her proposition out of the goodness of my heart. It has to be the right business decision. I decide to put it to the gang tonight and see what they think.

I'm back at the flat, and Jane is getting me a glass of wine… I feel like I need it. I've told her about meeting with Linda.

"I don't believe it!" says Jane. "I mean, I can't believe that you guys are thinking of doing this. It's either a great idea or completely mad!"

"I think I'm completely mad to even consider it to be honest. I don't even like the woman!" I take the wine from Jane and sit down at the kitchen table.

"I know you think she's great but, well, I just find her pushy, overbearing… oh god Jane, what on earth am I doing? Why did I even say I'd think about it?"

"So, what are you going to do?" she asks, pouring herself a glass too.

"I really don't know. Maybe I should get everyone to take a vote tonight! Oh dear. What a mess."

"Well I think that you should tell her where to go!" says Nat. "I mean, who does she think she is? First she shouts at you, then she changes her tune? I smell a rat."

We are sitting around Jane's table and Stuart has just opened a bottle of Baileys to go with the coffee.

"Well, you really have to think about it Kate," Stuart says, pouring out the Baileys, "and you should check her out, I mean financially. Make sure she's solid."

"Well I get a strange vibe from Linda to be frank," says Beth, waving her hands about in her theatrical way. "I think she's very insecure deep down, but maybe with time she'll be more confident and open up."

"The other thing to consider is if it would be better to have a business partner," says Stuart. "I don't know this woman, but if you think you could work with her it might be good to have someone to share the burden and the responsibility…"

"It's all good advice," I say. "I think I'm just going to have to sleep on it."

18

"Appear weak when you are strong, and strong when you are weak."

The Art of War, Sun Tzu

"Why on earth would you want a flat screen TV in a bookshop?" Linda is eyeing me across her cappuccino and for a moment looks stony-faced and unimpressed. We are sitting in a new, super cute little bar which has just opened around the corner from my place. It's called *Café per Due*. Manuela is the Italian owner – new to Panama, enthusiastic and superbly friendly. Within minutes I feel like I've known Manuela for years and I instantly feel I'll be a regular in here. The cappuccino is so good I'm soon on my second and wondering if I could justify a third. Manuela also does pizzas. They look mouthwatering and I'll probably be in here for lunch every day before you know it.

"I know it sounds weird but I was thinking that it would be really great to have a flat screen by the sofa. I'd like to have something really different in the shop, something completely unexpected and unique. So, I thought we could get a selection of those ambiance DVDs. You know, you can get reefs, log fires, country scenes, and waves crashing on the beach. I think it would be fun and make people really remember the shop. Give it a relaxing feel. Eventually we can also use it to feature and promote certain books on it too."

"Well, it's definitely different," she raises an eyebrow, takes a drag on her cigarette and blows the smoke a little too close in my direction. I can see that she's not convinced.

Two weeks have passed since I agreed to go into business with Linda and I had hoped that she'd grow on me. She is, slowly, that is for sure, but she's always on her guard, never letting her reserve down, always has an opinion and never fails to tell me. Then suddenly out of the blue she seems keen to bring me into her confidence.

Today she's more relaxed than I've ever seen her, telling me about the plastic surgery she's had done since arriving in Panama. I'm soon well informed about her eye lift, Botox and the lipo she had on her behind. I wanted to tell her that I'd rather not hear all the gory detail but she seemed intent on telling me everything and then even got some pictures up on her phone to show me the post-operative bruises. But thankfully I was able to move her away from this topic and we are back to discussing the matter at hand – the bookshop.

As we share and discuss, it becomes clear that Linda is surprisingly, given her arty background, the more traditional and I want to be a bit more creative. Linda doesn't quite know how to react to some of my ideas and I can see that there could be a few battles ahead.

I know, you're probably wondering why I've even decided to go into business with Linda. But you know, thinking about doing it all on my own – after I thought it through – it just made more sense to take on the burden with someone else. Not only that but the unit next to ours came up for rent recently. Linda scoped it out and she's now got the idea of opening an art gallery space in there. She tells me she can keep her old US business going a bit longer, and import art from the US while also featuring local artists, and that eventually it would be great to have our bookshop next door perhaps even physically linked to the gallery. I must admit I loved this idea. And Linda seemed so fired-up by it that I think eventually she'll focus more on that than the bookshop. She even said so in so many words. So, in that way I can get the best of both worlds: have a reliable partner in the bookshop, get to do it mainly my way and also have the benefit of a linked art gallery and bookshop bringing in even more potential customers – of exactly the right target for selling books to. Win, win.

I took Linda to see Jimmy's uncle's place, now my place, last week, and she loved it but I won't lie – even with the longer game plan of the gallery in mind, at times it was difficult to have this project until now wholly mine, shared with Linda. Her overflow of emotion, her ideas about how to construct and organize the shelves, where the counter and till should be and what type of sofas we should have to encourage people to stay, to browse, to read and to buy.

Linda is obviously not going to be content to take a back seat in this retail "complete beginners" course, at least until her gallery project is up and running. At times, I could hardly get a word in and had to battle and persist as she interrupted, talked over me and generally steam-rolled her way around the shop. I'm getting the feeling that she will want to have her say on much of the detail and that we might disagree on quite a bit of it: I said I'd like cream walls, she suggested something bright and colorful. I want white shelves, she wants wood. I want a new modern counter and till, she prefers something old and wooden. And so here we are, back with our coffee trying to hammer it out and coming up against our differences. But somehow, in spite of this, I think we're going to make it work. Something tells me. I can just sense it.

And at least the hard-core business arrangement that will be the drafting board of our hoped-for success has been agreed. I didn't want to leave this book open, I wanted it firmly read, understood and closed so that we can move on with hopefully the fun part of the shop. And somehow, we did. We decided eventually that we will work equal hours, put in equal amount of second-hand stock, and that I will take slightly more profit, as the shop is my investment, Linda isn't paying rent or hasn't had to invest in buying the space so for every book sold, I get 65 percent and she 35 percent. It seems fair, it seems right and we are both happy to review this arrangement in a few months' time. Everything else we will share; decisions on what stock, how to organize the shop, buying furniture – everything 50/50. Then it was on to what was supposed to be the fun stuff, meeting with our interior architect, going over to the shop and going through his plans.

Tomorrow we have to discuss the stock we want to buy, how to do it and most importantly – what stock. We need to make up lists and lists on my laptop of what we'd like to have in the shop, which authors, which bestsellers, which classics, and recent new titles. The lists are going to be endless and it should be fun.

As I'm staring at Linda across my cappuccino, my mind darts to my days in London spent behind a computer writing my "To do" list for a forthcoming charity event or telethon. And I feel a sense of freedom and relief that I'm here, not back in that world. For now, any disagreements I might have with Linda are minor worries compared to the grind of a nine to five in London.

"Well, I guess if you want this flat screen TV I can live with it," she says almost with a smile, indicating to Manuela for the bill.

"And tomorrow we're set for 2pm at yours to go over stock, right?" she asks, putting her cigarettes and lighter away in her bag.

I'm sure Linda and I can come to a mutual agreement over stock. After all, we're both well read; we'll both be more than willing to compromise there for sure.

"No, Kate, I'm sorry, that's never going to sell in Panama. I know you think that the list is limited, but we'll simply sell more books like John Grisham, Stephen King, that type of thing. Nobody's heard of half of the authors you're suggesting! They're only well known in England. For example, who's this Kate, Kate Atkinson? I've never heard of her!"

I'm beginning to feel my blood boil and it's not the heat although today is particularly hot. We're sitting at the kitchen table in my place, the air conditioning is on full blast but it's not cooling my temper. Tina, my cleaner, is sweeping the living room floor. She's making the strangest humming sounds. From time to time we are both distracted by her strange moaning. At first, I thought there was something wrong but then I see that she's plugged into the personal radio and her hips are swaying in time to some silent salsa beat and I realize that Tina is not in pain. She doesn't have a bad tooth ache; no doctor's appointment is required – it's just her favorite salsa track on the radio.

I take a deep breath and decide to postpone trying to explain to Linda 1) what a wonderful author Kate Atkinson is 2) how her book *Behind the Scenes at the Museum* is one of my all-time favorites and how 3) there's no way I'm not having Kate Atkinson in the stock. I decide to lose some battles in order to win the war and then also make a mental note to add it to the list later when she's not looking. I'm a sneak and I know it but today I just don't care.

We review the list again and again, deleting, adding, arguing, trying to balance, keeping an open mind and trying not to be swayed by what we like to read but what the customer would like, but it's hard. We've already decided we'd like to stock a really well thought out, personal choice of books, but it can't be too personal. It's not a bookshop for us. Linda is making a trip to the States next week to do some research, to see what's being stocked in bookshops in New York right now, and to meet up with some book sellers who might be able to supply us.

She's also going to meet up with Megan while she's there. I'm so envious I could burst, but there's far too much for us to do here – we can't both go. I have to be here to keep an eye on the shop.

That afternoon I take a walk over to see how the re-modeling is coming along. As I walk into the place I get a rush of excitement. The place is a hive of activity. The shelves are already going up and it's finally starting to look like a shop. The floor is down and a workman is painting one of the walls a rich orange color (Linda got her way on that one). I have to admit, the white shelves look great against it (I got my way on that one) and another workman, a carpenter, is building the counter (we couldn't find an antique counter so we've compromised and are having one built in wood).

Over the excitement, however, I'm suddenly overwhelmed by how much shelf-space there is. We've got so many shelves to fill – it is daunting. My second-hand stock and Linda's together will only fill about a third of the current shelves – meaning we have to fill the remaining space with new books. I try to not panic – not only over this undertaking, but also the investment we both need to put in. I wander over to take a look at the lounge area. This space is at the front by the windows. It's a good-sized space and we can fit a sofa and two armchairs here no problem. Then at the back of the shop, what was the small kitchen has been sectioned off so that there is also now a small office and stock room. It's small, but big enough for what we'll need. I take a deep breath and look around again. It's coming along nicely, very nicely indeed.

"Wow, I don't believe it!" I turn around and see Jimmy at the door, wide eyed and beaming. I haven't seen Jimmy in weeks. His trip to China had been extended and he's been gone for what seems a lifetime. Now he's standing at the door and for a moment I have to admit I didn't recognize him. He's sporting a trendy new "out of bed" haircut, wearing some very stylish jeans and a very flattering black t-shirt. In an instant I realize that Jimmy is actually a pretty good-looking guy. He seems more mature and, dare I say, *sexier* than I've ever remembered in the past. Attempting to put this thought to the back of my mind, through a fierce blush, which I hope he doesn't notice, I go over and give him a strangely self-conscious kiss on both cheeks.

"Kate, it's just fab!" he says giving me a kiss back. "I can't believe that this is the same place! Really, just to think, this is where I used to come for noodles when I was a kid. I don't believe it! When are you going to get all your stock in?" He's wandering around taking it all in.

"Well, next week for the second-hand, and in about a month for the new stock. That takes time. We still haven't ordered anything, but Linda is going up to New York to get working on it next week. So, you like the shop?"

"Kate, it's going to be great. What's going in that space?"

"Well, over there we'll have a sofa and a couple of armchairs and over here some tables with best sellers, recommendations. By the entrance, a stand on books related to Panama, travel guides that type of thing. And in this section, we'll have some language books, especially Spanish."

"Very well thought out," he says, nodding his approval. "I'm not a reader Kate, but maybe you'll turn me into one!"

"Then here there'll be fiction, over there history, current affairs. On these shelves self-help, religion, and here cookery, interior design, that type of thing."

"Well, you've got it pretty well planned. And that's second-hand over there, right?"

"Sure, that's second hand," I nod, running my eyes over the now empty shelves.

He's right; I can see it all so clearly. I have been dreaming it, seeing it in my sleep, with my eyes closed. Everywhere I look, I see categories, authors, hardbacks, paperbacks, fiction and non-fiction. I know every inch, where everything is going to be and how to stack the shelves so that it looks full, interesting, and irresistible. I can't wait to get started, to be surrounded by boxes of stock. I wish Megan could be here for that.

"So, how was your trip to China, Jimmy, and when did you get back?"

"Oh, I've been back a couple of days Kate, but look, I didn't forget, and got that appointment with the local authority, you remember, I mentioned it in the email."

Jimmy is amazing. Even on a business trip to China, he's been thinking of me, trying to help, calling people in the local authority he knows to try and get my documents and permits through.

"Thanks, so much Jimmy! I owe you a beer, or maybe a few!" I say, wondering when we'll be able to get together for something more sociable. Just the two of us would be nice…

"No problem Kate, I'm happy to help. I just love seeing new businesses get started. It makes me happy to see this old place getting transformed.

"So, anyway Kate, I was in the area so just popped by to see you and to tell you that tomorrow we have that appointment at the ministry of commerce about the permit and everything. If I come and get you tomorrow at 9.30 is that OK?"

"Sure, I'll be ready. Do you think it will be OK? I mean, I know that these things normally take ages and we really want to open in a month if possible, to make the most of the tourist season while it lasts." We'd already noticed tour groups passing through *Casco Viejo* each day – most likely tourists off the many visiting cruise ships passing through. Some parties had even stopped outside the shop and had pressed their noses against the glass to look inside. I was convinced that if we'd been open, some would have come in and we would have made sales.

"Don't worry; it'll be no problem. You'll be sorted out in five minutes," he says grinning and then his phone is ringing again and he's gone before I can even say goodbye.

Jimmy picks me up the next morning and looks just as stylish. I can't help wondering if he's had a bit of a makeover in China or if I've just never noticed before now. While I'm musing on this we glide through the streets in his smooth, leather seated fully air-conditioned sports car. It's a welcome change to the taxi rides I normally take where the taxi is often almost falling apart and salsa blasting on the stereo. Jimmy has a little light jazz playing and I've got to admit to myself that I might just be becoming attracted to this young Panamanian Chinese guy.

"So, you like jazz?" I ask taking him in from the passenger seat while he carefully maneuvers through the busy, congested rush hour traffic.

"Who me? Yeah, I really like jazz. I've been into it since I was about 18."

"But you don't hear much jazz in Panama. It seems that people in Panama are mostly into salsa." He smiles and glances over as he drives.

"Well, you know Kate, I've never been mad on salsa. I mean I like some salsa artists but there's more out there than just salsa. To be honest I prefer jazz. You know there's quite a jazz scene here in Panama, right? I got into it when I was 18. I went down to *Casco Viejo* one night. I didn't know it was the Panama Jazz festival. You know all the streets are closed to traffic and they set up a stage in the main square. It's every January. I remember it now. There was a really good band on and I was just mesmerized by it all. Anyway, since then I started collecting jazz and I've got quite a big CD collection. You should come over and see it sometime." He glances over and smiles again, and once more I suddenly feel myself blushing.

"Of course, these last few years I'm downloading music more and more... here we are," he said breaking my flow of thoughts as we pull into a crowded car park and he deftly finds a spot near the entrance.

"Let's get this paper work done! My friend has helped me with a number of things to do with the restaurant, so it shouldn't be a problem at all."

"Three months!" I'm almost in tears. Jimmy is standing by the car, hands on his hips and looking sheepish.

"I'm sorry, Kate. I really thought my friend would be able to help. I really didn't realize that he'd been transferred to a different department."

I'm devastated. Three months to wait for the permit is a huge setback, but I certainly can't blame Jimmy, he's only been trying to help.

"Jimmy, really, it's hardly your fault! I should've been onto this a lot sooner. I've only got myself to blame. I don't know how I'm going to tell Linda. She's going to flip."

"Let's go get a coffee," he says beckoning me over to the car.

We drive to a nearby coffee bar, park the car and make a beeline for the air-conditioned interior. Jimmy soon has two coffees ordered and we sit down by the window overlooking the sea. For a moment, I'm lost in thought and feel myself sinking into a real low about the permit.

"Look Kate, I know that this is really bad news but let's try and look on the positive. Having more time will enable you to really get the shop ready with no stress. You were just saying the other day that you were beginning to feel the strain. Three months isn't that long, is it?"

"I know what you mean; it's just that we really wanted to get open before the tourist season ends to make the most of it while all the tourists will be around. In three months, it'll almost be at and end an we'll have missed out on so much business."

"Oh, I hadn't thought of that," he said looking deflated.

"Well, I guess there's nothing we can do," I say smiling and trying to put a brave face on it for Jimmy.

"Kate, if there's anything else I can do, you just ask, OK?" he says taking a spoon to measure in some sugar.

"Jimmy, thanks, you know you've already been a great help. I mean I wouldn't have the shop at all if it wasn't for you."

Jimmy looks down into his coffee and stirs it slowly. For a moment he seems lost in his own thoughts.

"Well, you know Kate; I guess I had a vested interest in getting you to stay." He looks up and fixes my gaze. "After all, it's kind of nice having you around." For a second, I can't move. What is Jimmy saying? Is he just being kind, friendly or is there something deeper in this comment. My stomach suddenly lurches and I feel ever so slightly nauseous.

"Well Jimmy, that's very nice of you to say. You know that I'm glad that I decided to come back, that I could buy your uncle's shop."

"You know Kate, I really admire you," he says with a very earnest look on his face. "You decided you wanted the shop, came back and did it."

"Well, I haven't done it yet," I say, smiling. "It could all come crashing down yet."

"I don't think so Kate. You're too determined, and I admire that. You know all the Panamanian girls I meet are so, so boring. They all want to find a guy who's going to look after them and do all the work. I much prefer the American, European approach where the woman is an equal partner in the relationship. When I get married, I want someone who I can come home to and share my day with, ask advice. I don't want to be the one who's calling all the shots all the time."

"That's kind of fair," I say and for a moment I get the urge to reach out and take his hand, but then the waitress comes over and the moment is gone and thank goodness! I could've made a real fool of myself.

Jimmy drops me back at *Casco Viejo* and as he drives away I can't help wondering what's going on. I think my imagination is running riot and that I misread Jimmy and his comments. He's just fond of me and glad that I stuck around. After all, he'd be interested in someone far more glamorous than me. I saw photos of his ex-girlfriend and she was stunning. Now I have to push thoughts of Jimmy out of my mind and tell Linda the bad news. She's not going to be happy.

19

I struggle with another box of second-hand books. The air conditioning hasn't been installed yet and it's boiling in here. Every day I call the air conditioner guy and he promises to turn up but never does. It's so frustrating. I wipe the perspiration from my forehead and just as I do, I feel a bead of sweat trickle down my back. It feels like my body is oozing sweat from every pore. If I don't take a shower in the next few hours I'll smell like a monkey's armpit. Not only that, but if I go on much longer like this without a drink I'll shrivel up like one of those dried apricots you see in the health food shops.

Linda has been gone a week and I'm sure she's having a much better time meeting with suppliers, having coffee with Megan, generally enjoying herself in New York. And here I'm left humping heavy boxes around and stocking shelves. Somehow, I seemed to have drawn the short straw on that one. The shelves for second-hand books are almost half done but it is painstaking work, putting all the fiction into alphabetical order, organizing the various non-fiction sections, logging the stock on the computer, but in spite of all this hard work, I'm loving every minute. I'm tired today though and decide to take a break and maybe even call it a day. It's already almost 7pm, it's Friday and I've been working like crazy for a week.

I grab my bag, lock up the shop and decide to head over to Bar Blanca to see if anyone is around. After all, it is the weekend now and with a bit of luck the evening might just fall into place and take care of itself. The breeze is refreshing in the indigo of the early evening and as I enter the square, I immediately see Stuart sitting at one of the many tables, lit up by a yellow street lamp. He's having an animated conversation on the phone. He sees me and waves me over, points repeatedly at the chair next to him and grins. I pull out the chair and sit down. While he manically chats on the phone, I order an Electric Lemonade from Ricky, who just happens to be passing my table with a big, carefree grin.

"Sorry about that," Stuart finally says, putting his phone down, leaning over and giving me a kiss on the cheek.

"I've just got a really impressive potential investor interested in New York – could be worth $4 million for the fund." He's beaming and is waving over Ricky for what I'm guessing by the empty table in front of him is his first drink of the evening.

"Then, I've just completed on a building here in *Casco Viejo* which I'm going to develop into flats."

"Wow, you kept that one quiet Stuart! When did that go through?" I can see Stuart doing well with this. He's got property on the brain.

"Well, I spotted the place around three months ago. I didn't want to mention it to anyone until it was a dead cert. It's almost falling down but with some serious development it could make me a lot of money. I mean, you know about the prices in *Casco*…"

"Stuart! Not that again. Please, let's talk about something else."

"Oh, do we have to!" he says in a mock disappointed voice.

"Well we could try!" I say laughing.

"Anyway, Kate, good timing, I literally just sat down here myself when I spotted you. How's the shop going?"

It strikes me that I'm probably becoming as single-minded as Stuart. He's obsessed with making money on property and investments, me on my shop. I must be so boring these days.

"Well, it's coming along just great, except one thing, but then once I've told you about that, can we agree to talk about something other than property or my shop?"

"Sure!" he says laughing, "but first, tell me what the problem is."

I fill Stuart in on all the details of the permit and he sips his Electric Lemonade looking thoughtful.

"Wish I could help you Kate, but I'm afraid I don't know anyone in that governmental department. I wish I did."

"So," I say, quickly trying to change the subject, suddenly feeling more than bored with the endless string of problems I seem to face. "What have you been up to recently, Stuart, apart from making your millions, of course?"

This is becoming a familiar pastime with Stuart. Cocktails, long conversation, a lot of laughing, too, especially after the second cocktail. Before long, I'm listening to Stuart tell me about a friend of his, who's started seeing a Panamanian guy.

"... so, I told her, I said, he's not got much upstairs, but never mind, he's bloody good-looking and he's got an amazing body," Stuart laughs to himself sucking on the straw, his face screwing up in concentration as he tries to get as much as possible out of the bottom of the glass. The little red umbrella in the cocktail knocks against his nose and for a second, he looks quite comical.

"Hey, want another?" he asks, giving up on that one.

"Stuart, can I ask you something? It's a bit personal."

"Oh, I like the sound of that!" he says grinning. "Shoot."

"Well, it's very personal, actually."

"Come on Kate, spit it out! What are you going to ask me, like if I'm gay or something?"

For a moment I'm stunned. How did he guess, he's just joking around but he's hit the nail on the head. I suddenly feel very embarrassed and ashamed. He leans over grinning.

"You're not the first person to ask and probably won't be the last but well, maybe I thought you of all people might have been able to work it out…"

"Well, no… not really, you see…"

"Kate, don't you get it?" he asks, getting more serious all of a sudden.

"Get what, Stuart?" I'm baffled, lost and really don't know what on earth he's going on about.

"Why do you think I hang out in *Casco Viejo* all the time?"

"Because, err, you like it?" I say carefully. Is this a trick question? I'm just not getting it.

"Well, yes but there's another reason. I never used to hang out here so much…"

I'm racking my brains. Actually, come to mention it, Stuart is in *Casco* a lot. I assumed that he likes it and has always hung out here, but actually he lives on the other side of Panama City. I guess this is a bit out of his way, but then Jane, Beth and Nat live here too.

"Well, I just thought that all your friends live round here, so of course you're going to hang out here…" I say.

"Sure, my friends live around here Kate, but, well, isn't it obvious? There's one person in particular I hope to see when I come to *Casco*…"

Stuart has fixed me with his eyes and is confidently smiling across the table. He picks up his cocktail and takes another sip, waiting for this bombshell to sink in. For a moment I'm at a loss about what to think, but then a wave of anticipation catches me unawares and I blush, it feels like from my finger tips to my nose.

"Oh, I see," I say hesitating, trying to grope for the right answer. I'm not at all sure what that is. I'm still not sure if I've misunderstood. I don't want to make a fool of myself but something inside tells me that I've picked up the right message. Stuart has been growing on me. He's good-looking, fun and if he can stop talking investments for a second full of interesting conversation.

"Look, I'm really sorry about asking you. I mean about the gay thing," I say, suddenly feeling like a complete fool.

"Well, like I said, you're not the first to ask me if I'm gay Kate, so I'm not surprised. You know I don't date very often. I'm very choosy and some people think that's strange and a sign that I'm gay or something and, I guess I'm also very in tune with my feminine side. That's why I'm a great catch!

"Fancy another drink?"

"Why not!" I say, wondering where things are going to lead from here.

"And, can I buy you dinner tonight?" he asks, looking back at me while he waves over to get Ricky's attention.

"That would be lovely!" I smile back. Looks like my night has suddenly taken an unexpected turn.

"Hey, now what's this I hear about you and Stuart dating?" I'm at Beth's office with Jane who's helping me with an advert which Beth has offered to put in her *Panorama* magazine. It's great to get some free publicity. The shop is opening in two weeks' time and *Panorama* is hugely popular.

A monthly glossy with a combination of what's on plus more in-depth features on local issues, interviews with local entrepreneurs, places to visit, restaurant reviews and the like – it's the go to magazine in Panama for ex-pats. Beth has promised to do a feature on the bookshop, once it's up and running, too.

"Who told you that?" I ask indignantly. Seems you can't be seen here too often with the same person or people start talking.

"Well, May mentioned that you've been spotted with Stuart a lot this week and it doesn't take much to put two and two together," she says cheekily, obviously fishing for information.

"And come up with five!" I finish. I know this place is small but good grief, you can't do anything here without everyone noticing. OK, I admit Stuart and I have been "hanging out" a lot this week but I wouldn't call it dating. Oh, apart from the kiss on my balcony last night, and then the night before we did have a kind of romantic dinner with candles, but that doesn't mean we're dating, does it?

"Look Jane, we're just kind of going out a bit and getting to know each other. It's not like we're an item or anything. We don't really know each other and, well, after what happened with Marco I'm taking it very slowly."

"Does Stuart understand that? I mean the taking it slowly bit?" she says with a grin.

"What do you mean?" I ask, feeling suddenly uncertain about where this conversation is going.

"Well, to be honest Kate, I haven't seen Stuart with a woman since arriving in Panama," she continues while she concentrates on the advert. "And I get the impression that he's a very single-minded person. You know what he's like, once he's made his mind up, there's no stopping him. Look how he's come down here and is already making stacks of money. There was an article in the local paper about him the other day. I think he's going to be seriously rich very soon. Especially now that the fund seems to be really taking off. He was even talking about fund number 2 the other day."

"Well I don't know about all that," I say. I'm almost irritated now. After all, this has nothing to do with anyone else. Why are they so nosy? I know they are my friends but…

"Look Kate, we're just happy for you, aren't we, Beth?" says Jane, glancing over at Beth who is working on a feature at the next computer.

"My dear, we just want you to be happy and at peace. Stuart is a great guy and there's nothing wrong with having a bit of fun too," says Beth in her calm laidback manner from the next desk.

"Now, what about Jimmy?" asks Jane with a wicked grin. "I kind of had you and him making a superb couple. He's cute, interesting, sensitive, very loyal."

"Well, yes I guess I had noticed that he's cute," I say, blushing, which of course is like showing a red rag to a bull.

"Oh!!!! So, you quite like Jimmy, too?" she says laughing, "oh god, things are going to get seriously interesting around here. Wow Kate, you're a real dark horse. If I wasn't taken I'd suggest we go out man hunting together sometime soon! And what about that guy you met in New York, the barman, the writer guy. What happened to him? He sounded really nice. What was he called? Paul?"

"Oh Pete?" I say, thinking back to New York with a bit of a pang. Pete had written to me a couple of times. He'd even tried to invite himself down. I immediately wrote back and said that of course he was welcome once I was settled but then I never got back in touch.

"Well, we kind of lost touch, I guess," I say without going into all the details. Actually, come to mention it, why had I let that one drift away, fizzle out. He was super nice, and really cute, too, thinking about it now...

"Well, Kate, you really are getting the attention it seems. They always say the quiet ones are the worst!" Jane laughs.

Just then, there is a knock at the door and May arrives with Paco. After giving some cuddles to Paco we go back to the computer.

"So, what's this I hear about you and Stuart?" asks May.

"What!?" I exclaim, feeling like my private life is not very private after all.

"Don't go there May," grins Jane. "We just went over all that. She's not spilling the beans."

"No comment, May. But what about you?" I say, smiling and deflecting the conversation back. "What about someone for you? Have you met anyone special recently?"

"Oh, I'm a hopeless case," she says, looking deflated and taking a swig at what must have been a very warm can of Coke she was carrying around and flopping on a nearby armchair.

"I've been here over a year and haven't seen one guy I'd be

remotely interested in. Mind you, it wasn't much better in New York. It seems like there are cute guys everywhere but then they're either afraid to commit, already with someone, or gay!"

"So, how's this looking?" says Jane, bringing our thoughts back to the advert.

"And what about you, Beth. Is that OK with you?"

Beth and May come over and we all lean across the table to get a better look at the computer screen. Jane had done a course in graphic design just after college and has managed to put together a very professional-looking advert using a photo I'd taken of the front of the shop.

"Wow, it's great! Thanks, so much Jane!" I exclaim in excitement and feeling suddenly pretty proud too.

"Well, if things don't work out with Stuart, you can pay me back by having a girls' night out and I can pretend to be single again," she says smiling up.

20

"Good friends, good books and a sleepy conscience: this is the ideal life."

Mark Twain

The bookshop is opening tonight and I thought I would be a nervous wreck, but I'm not, I'm just plain happy. It has taken quite some getting here, but here I am – The Bookshop of Panama is finally opening its doors to the public. It's marvelous.

Linda and I have been getting on much better, too. It's kind of come out of nowhere. Bit by bit she seems to have calmed down, like she doesn't have anything to prove any longer. We've even been sharing a joke and, strange as it may sound, we've even got quite a similar sense of humor.

"... so, then I told him that a homeless guy had taken his Armani suits out of the garbage bin!" I finish. Linda almost doubles up, letting out a huge howl of laughter. Marco has become a bit of a butt of our jokes. Now that I feel well and truly over him, it's quite good fun taking the piss out of Mr. UN Action Man. And I know I'm over him. I can say that now after he turned up here the other day.

I was on my own in the shop, putting some final touches to the cookery section. We'd had a recent delivery from the US including

Jamie Oliver's latest bestseller and I had somehow gotten a little waylaid skimming through it, including the pasta section at the back of the book.

It really was a beautiful book, with great looking recipes and big colorful pictures and I was completely engrossed in it. I hadn't even glanced up when a huge crack of thunder exploded above the piazza outside, followed by repeated flashes of white lightning. It was that time of year. Violent electrical storms were part and parcel of this tropical climate – I'd come to love them.

The rain was pelting down. I could hear it against the window. The raindrops sounded like small rubber bullets. Then suddenly, almost in my subconscious, I heard a tapping, a knocking on what sounded like the glass of the door. Looking up, I saw him. Marco. He was standing outside peering in, sheltering under a big cherry red umbrella. My first impression was that he looked great, and leaner than before. He was wearing jeans and a fitted t-shirt. It made him look toned and really in shape. Funny, I hadn't noticed that before – when I was dating him, that is – the muscles in his arms. Had he been working out?

For what seemed like minutes, although it was probably only a second or two, we fixed each other's gaze through the glass panes of the door. Then, he motioned to ask if he could come in and I came out of my trance and jumped up to get the door.

"Hi, Kate, how are you?" he asked, gingerly stepping into the shop and shaking his umbrella outside onto the pavement. He propped it up, dripping by the door. "It has been a while," he said turning around to face me.

"It sure has," I said, trying to maintain my calm composure while my stomach lurched inside. What the bloody hell was he doing here?!

"I hope you don't mind me passing by. I've been in Panama for three days for a regional workshop and, well, someone from the local office mentioned this new bookshop and then suddenly your name came up. Goes to show what a small place this is, and well,

I couldn't believe it to be honest, I'd just assumed you'd have left months ago and would be back in London... I just didn't think for a minute that you'd be here, still here, and doing this..." he looked around and took in the shop, nodding his approval.

"Wow, Kate, I have to say this is really impressive. Is this really your place, your bookshop?"

"Sure, it's mine," I said eyeing him up. "Why, is that so strange?"

"Well, I didn't think you'd..."

"Have it in me? Be adventurous enough? Have the nerve?" I gave back to him, beginning to feel annoyed.

"Well no, I didn't mean that, Kate," he said a bit sheepishly, "Just that you seemed to have a life plan and that plan was London, the office and weekends reading, your head buried in a book..."

"Good grief, is that how you saw me?" I said feeling shocked.

"No," he said almost kindly, "I didn't mean that, god, me and my mouth... just that, look I guess I'm really glad you've done something with your passion, with books. It takes some balls to do this – set up a business. I'm impressed."

"What are you doing here Marco? What do you want?" I said starting to feel more than irritated. I mean, just turning up out of the blue like this after what he pulled...

"I... when I heard you were here... I just wanted to see you, to say I'm truly sorry for what happened, to make sure that you're OK. You look great by the way. Panama obviously suits you..."

"And how's the wife?" I said, cutting in but without even a note of bitterness that almost surprised me.

"Candice? Oh, well, that didn't last, actually we never got married. She re-thought the whole thing, the field, getting married, me... I think she's working in Tokyo now as a special advisor to the UN Representative there. We're not even in touch anymore." Did I see a slight flush of red on his cheeks?

"So, she dumped you?" I said, trying not to sound smug.

"Well, if you put it like that... yes, she dumped me," he said shifting uncomfortably on his feet. For a second, I was tempted to say "poetic justice" or "karma" or "what goes around comes around", something like that but didn't. I didn't feel happy, I didn't feel sad. I realized right there that I didn't feel anything for Marco at all. My lack of feeling was a great feeling, if you know what I mean.

"Well Marco, it's been great to see you but I have a lot to do," I said, gesturing to the piles of books on the floor. "And as you can see, I'm fine, really good actually. You shouldn't feel guilty at all.

"In fact, you dumping me turned out really well – for me that is. If it hadn't happened, I might never have done this, opened a bookshop. So really, no problem. Thanks for stopping by. I appreciate the gesture and look… the shop is opening tomorrow. If you're still in town, you're more than welcome to pass by, there'll be a band in the square just outside here, drinks – a good Italian friend who owns the café around the corner is providing the pizza…"

"I'm flying out tonight Kate, so won't be able to make it but, anyway, thanks for the invite and for being so, so reasonable. It's been great to see you, see you doing so well, I hope we can be… friends… once again I really am so sorry for what happened and for the way it happened. I hope you can forgive me deep down, and, you take care of yourself…"

And with that, he headed for the door. Just before he left, hand on the door handle, he turned around.

"By the way, that email you sent me, about the homeless guy finding my Armani suits, was it true?"

"Sure, every word," I said.

He grinned, "You know, I wasn't sure at the time, but well, it brought a smile to my face." And with that, he was out the door. I watched the cherry red umbrella across the piazza through the rain and finally it disappeared from sight around a corner on the other side of the square.

"Oh my god, what the hell…!" I said to myself, sitting down suddenly on the nearest armchair.

"I need a drink!"

21

"Where is human nature so weak as in the bookstore."

Henry Ward Beecher

The salsa band is in full swing outside in the piazza and a crowd has gathered. Some people are already pairing up and beginning to get into the swing of it. The atmosphere is warm and friendly. There are local Panamanians from the square, tourists, ex-pats – a real mixed bag. It seems to sum up the cocktail that is Panama entirely. Thankfully it's not raining although nothing could dampen my spirits right now. The shop is crowded and the wine is flowing. The pizza has already been devoured and Manuela has gone back to *Café per Due* to put in a repeat order – another 20 pizzas should keep the pizza chef busy and our customers and friends happy.

Linda is on the till and sales are going down a storm, especially the new books. It was a good move to not only stock second-hand books. Everyone wants new releases and *New York Times* best sellers. Seems like Linda has more business sense than I'd given her credit for at the beginning. She's really done well with the stock selection and I'm hoping we don't run out of some of the more popular books. I can already see that the latest John Grisham is flying off the shelves fast.

I'm taking some time away from the till, chatting to Stuart while Linda is in control. I should make it clear – Stuart and me – we are most definitely *not* an item. We had a few dates and for a moment, it looked like we could end up in the sack together but, well, it just wasn't working for me. I just couldn't get over the fact that Stuart is more like a brother than anything else. I don't have a brother but kissing him felt like he was my brother and was just wrong. Stuart's a great friend and that's where it'll rest.

Seems Stuart is fine with that, too. At first, I thought things might be really strange between us; normally they would, but we seem to have slotted right back into how it was before. And secretly I still suspect that Stuart might be gay or bisexual, but just doesn't know it. Jane was really surprised when she found out we weren't really an item. I guess she secretly hoped we were going to end up married or something, but she soon moved on to a new prospect – me and Jimmy. I never would've guessed that she was such a matchmaker.

But since the day when Jimmy and I went to get the permits for the shop, there's been no hint of anything from Jimmy. No sign of interest in me at all. In fact, more the opposite. He's started dating the most gorgeous woman, half Panamanian half Chinese and it looks like Jimmy is well and truly smitten. He's over in the corner with her now. Over two glasses of wine they are completely oblivious to everyone else and it's like live sparks are flying between them.

In all honesty in the beginning, I was a little disappointed, but after a week of feeling low I'm just happy for them now. After all, Jimmy was too young for me and I don't think he was ever really interested in me in any case. Looking at how beautiful Rosa is, I'm not surprised. He's got amazing taste. Not only is she beautiful she's also super intelligent, professionally successful – has her own interior design business – and is very well read. An added bonus for me is that Rosa and I really hit it off and I think we might become good friends.

The evening is going swimmingly, just one blot on the horizon, Megan. She was supposed to be here but she isn't. Instead she's in hospital.

She was supposed to arrive last night but at about 6pm I got a call from her neighbor. She had collapsed that morning in the hall outside her flat and an ambulance had rushed her to hospital. I was about to cancel the whole opening and go up to New York but word came back quite quickly that the hospital had run all the tests and seems that it's just a virus. Megan will be fine. She just needs a few days in hospital and then she'll be home and she should be as right as rain.

"No Kate, I really insist. I will be so very angry if you cancel the opening for me! I'm fine. In fact, strangely with all the drugs they're pumping into me I've never felt better. And listen, good news on the ticket. Due to the circumstances the airline is willing to book me on another flight in the future for a very small re-booking fee, so I don't completely lose the ticket. I'll be down to Panama to see you before you can blink!"

"Are you sure Megan?" I asked with a huge dollop of uncertainty probably sounding down the phone.

"Yes! Now don't insist, Kate. But there is something I wanted to mention to you... you remember Pete?"

Pete, how could I forget Pete. We'd spent some lovely time together in New York during those last days. He's an amazing guy and very cute too. Sometimes I wonder why nothing happened with him, but on reflection I don't think I was in any frame of mind for romance. I was in such a hyper state about going back to Panama and not completely over Marco.

But now, hearing Megan talk about Pete, I had to admit that a butterfly had just fluttered in my stomach – and suddenly, my interest had perked up. That, mixed together with pangs of guilt. He had sent me two or three messages on Facebook recently. He had obviously been trying to reach out, get in touch – I'd meant to write back, but well, somehow I just hadn't gotten around to it...

"Sure, I remember Pete, why?"

"Well, Kate, he got in touch with me recently. By the way he said he'd written to you a couple of times and was really hoping to hear back from you. Anyway, he just got published! It's wonderful. He's so excited, you can just imagine.

"I'm going to stock his book when it's out next year and he's going to do a reading and book signing too. Isn't it fabulous? Especially after all those times he got rejected by publishers – just goes to show. Well, anyway, I mentioned your bookshop, the opening and he said that it had been so long since he'd had a holiday and now that he was getting published he'd have the money and..."

The butterfly fluttered again. "What? You don't mean..."

"Well, to cut a long story short, he booked a ticket to Panama, too – we were going to come together – Pete, as a surprise! I encouraged him, of course, he really wasn't certain to begin with, especially as you haven't been in touch with him in a while.

"But I can be very persuasive, and anyway, I told him that it was just because you had been so busy with the shop and of course you wanted to see him. But as I'm not able to come myself I thought that maybe I should mention it now... I hope I did the right thing... anyway, at first when I spoke to him about being taken into hospital he was also going to cancel but then I said, I mean – why should he cancel too just because I can't make it? Well, as you can imagine then that took some more persuasion, but..."

"Oh my, well I'm glad you did tell me," I said, running my hands through my hair, and suddenly feeling a complete mess. I had never found time for the hairdresser. Thank goodness, I had an appointment for the next morning, the day of the opening. I really wanted to look my best.

"He's very excited to be coming, although he really seems a bit nervy about it. I can't imagine why. He's never been to Central America before, so maybe that's the reason, and then Kate, I promised I wouldn't say anything, but I think he holds a bit of a candle for you, Kate..."

We chatted a while longer and then I could hear the nurse telling Megan that she really shouldn't be using the phone so late and Megan said she had to go "to get my beauty sleep," she laughed.

After talking to Megan, I had gotten right on the computer and had written back to Pete. To tell him to come and that I was looking forward to seeing him. I don't know whether he saw the message as I didn't hear back. And now I have to admit, I've got butterflies. Pete, a guy I hardly know, is coming straight from the airport and will be here any minute.

My mind has been wandering. It's well after 9.30pm, the launch party is in full swing and Pete should've landed by now. He should be here soon. Linda and I have just had our photos taken outside the shop for the local press, the words "big fish, small pond" had come to mind, but hey, if we can get some free publicity that's great.

"Kate! How wonderful this is – I just can't believe it!" Beth and Nat have arrived. "You must be so proud!" They come over and each gives me kisses on both cheeks.

"And this is for you," says Beth, pushing something into my hand. "It's a North American Indian good-luck doll. You have to put it somewhere high up on the wall, like ideally over the entrance," she says. "It will ensure only happy things happen in this location." I take a closer look. It's a beautiful wooden doll with woolen hair. It looks hand painted and is very unusual. I don't think I've seen anything quite like it before.

"Thanks, so much Beth. It's lovely. Thanks, guys," I say, giving them both a hug.

"I've got five books here," says Jane, coming over while trying to balance the books in one hand with her wine in the other. "I'm going to get these – then, anyone for dancing?"

"Hey, Kate, I'm so glad that Chase can make it," she says, turning to me. "He's arriving late but looking at the crowd outside, it should all be still happening by the time he makes it. Last time I checked, his flight from Miami was still on time.

"Oh, that salsa band is great! They're the regulars from Jazz Point Jazz Club, right?" she asks, taking a sip of wine. If the pizza hadn't run out she'd probably be trying to balance a slice of that in her hand, too. I grab the books, which look like they are about to topple to the floor, and take them over to the counter where Linda is just finishing with a customer.

"They're great, no?" I say walking back. "We're really lucky to get them actually. They were fully booked, then at the last minute they had a cancelation – so we only knew that they could do it on Wednesday."

"Excellent," says Nat, bobbing his head in time to the salsa tune which is reaching us inside the shop from the square outside. "Time to party!" he says pulling Beth to the door and together they disappear into what is now quite a large crowd of people salsa dancing in the piazza.

And then I see him. Pete. At the door, suitcase trailing behind him. He's searching around, trying to find me.

"Pete!" I shout over the chatting crowd. He sees me and grins, a little uncertainly. Pulling his case behind him, he winds through the crowds to reach me.

"Hi Kate, it's… it's great to see you. You look wonderful! I hear Megan tipped you off – about my surprise star guest appearance." He smiles and before I know it we are hugging each other tightly. Pulling back to look at him, I remember his fragrance, his touch, the feel of his hand in mine. He looks great, new glasses I notice. They suit him.

"Pete, it's great to see you! Here; let's find somewhere for your suitcase. How was the trip?" Suddenly I feel nervous.

"There's something special for you in there," he says shyly as I take the case from his hand and take it over to the back of the shop to lock it safely away in the storeroom.

"Some proofing copies of my book…" And then before I know what's happened, right in the middle of the thriller section he's pulling me to him, kissing me on the lips and I find that I'm kissing him back.

"Pete, I'm sorry…" I say pulling back. "I mean, sorry about the Facebook messages, the emails. I'm so crap at staying in touch and…"

Suddenly, I can't understand why I haven't been emailing this guy every day. And, come to think about it, how come he's here? After all, I haven't exactly been giving him "interested" signals since leaving New York. Was I crazy!?

"You don't have anything to be sorry about." He strokes my hair and kisses me again. "I haven't been able to get you out of my mind since you left.

"I don't know what's wrong with me. I can obviously express myself in writing but, well, when it comes to picking up the phone, I don't know, I mean I should've called you to tell you just how I felt after you left but I didn't want to push you," he says, looking pained.

"But seeing you here, seeing you now… hell, I should be the one apologizing not you… I mean, for kissing you like this, just in the door too, it's just that my feelings overcame me and…" Now it's my turn and I kiss him back. He tastes amazing. His lips are soft but firm, his stubble just rough enough without hurting, his back sweaty through his shirt, but nice to touch.

Somewhere in the distance I think I can hear a salsa version of a classic Earth, Wind & Fire tune *"Boogie Wonderland"*. Jane's influence, no doubt. Only Jane could get a salsa band onto Earth, Wind & Fire. And somehow right there and then I know that everything is going to be fine.

Life is a funny twist and turn of a journey. London, Panama, New York, Panama. Where next? Logistically, Pete and I, well, we are hardly a match made in heaven – Pete in New York, me down here in Panama, but whatever happens I know deep down that things are going to work out, and that maybe, just maybe whatever happens, The Bookshop of Panama will be fine… and it's strange, I would never have imagined it but that salsa version of *Boogie Wonderland* drifting in from the square right now, somehow, strangely does seem to work.

"Fancy a dance?" I ask. Pete gazes out into the square and back at me. The sound of the band whafts through to the back of the shop along with the sound of laughter. He squeezes me tight. His arms are surprisingly strong.

"I thought you were never going to ask," he grins.

With credit: GettyImages/stevedangers

From Kate's Panama Scrapbook:

Sancocho Soup for 4

- *1 chicken cut into pieces*
- *1 tablespoon oil*
- *3 garlic cloves pressed*
- *2 tablespoons fresh oregano*
- *4 tablespoons fresh coriander*
- *1 large onion chopped*
- *1.3 kilograms of yuca/cassava*

1. *Season the chicken with the garlic, oregano, and pepper.*
2. *Brown the seasoned chicken in a large heavy pot in the oil over a medium flame and allow to sweat.*
3. *Setting aside a little coriander for a garnish, add the rest of the coriander, onion and water.*
4. *Make sure water covers the chicken and bring to a boil then reduce to a low simmer for 20 minutes.*
5. *Meanwhile, cut the yucca into small chunks.*
6. *After the chicken has simmered for 20 minutes, add the yucca.*
7. *Cook for about 1 hour or until everything softens.*
8. *Keep adding water if necessary.*
9. *Stir in salt to taste.*
10. *Serve.*

Ceviche (lime marinated fish)

- *500 grams of sea bass*
- *Juice from 8 limes*
- *1 red onion chopped*
- *2–3 green chilies*
- *2–3 tomatoes chopped*
- *Bunch of coriander*
- *2 tbsp extra-virgin olive oil*
- *Pinch caster sugar*

1. *Combine the fish, lime juice and onion in a large bowl. The juice should completely cover the fish;*
2. *Cover with cling film and place in the fridge for some hours.*
3. *Add chilies, tomatoes, coriander and olive oil, stir gently. Remove any excess liquid, then season with a good pinch of salt and sugar.*

Electric Lemonade

4 Ingredients: Mix and put in lots of ice:

- *1 oz Vodka*
- *Sprite*
- *Sour Mix*
- *1/2 oz Blue Curacao*

ABOUT THE AUTHOR

Suzanne Hope grew up in Heysham Village, Lancashire, in the UK and studied history before launching a career in fundraising and marketing. Through her work for international organizations she has lived in Rome, Geneva, Bangkok and also spent two years in Panama. Here, inspired by the Central American setting, the colorful, eclectic ex-pats she met and her love of bookshops, she started writing and *The Bookshop of Panama* was born. She now lives in Brooklyn, New York, with her husband Francesco and two cats Mimi and Bunny. *The Bookshop of Panama* is her first novel.